TWO BIG
DIFFERENCES

a novel

BY IAN ROSS SINGLETON

Illustrated by William Ford

BOSTON · 2021

D1596098

IAN ROSS SINGLETON

Two Big Differences. *A Novel*

Edited by Josie Schoel

Copyright © 2021 by Ian Ross Singleton

ISBN 978-1950319619 (pbk)
Library of Congress Control Number: 2021946336

Book Design and Layout by M·GRAPHICS © 2021
Illustrations by William Ford © 2021

Published by M·GRAPHICS | Boston, MA

🖥 www.mgraphics-books.com
✉ mgraphics.books@gmail.com
   info@mgraphics-books.com

Printed in the United States of America

Одесса очень скверный город. Это всем известно. Вместо «большая разница» там говорят — «две большие разницы».

Odessa's a very wretched city. Everybody knows that. Instead of "a big difference," they say, "two big differences."

— **Isaak Babel (1894–1940)**

Изя, ты куда идешь? — Нет, иду домой.

Izya, where are you going? No, I'm going home.

— **Mikhail Zhvanetsky (1934–2020)**

PROLOGUE

VALENTINE, VALYA, OR VALINKA

This story is the American English version of one that should take place in Ukrainian Russian. Odessan Russian, Zina would say. She would call me Valinka or Valya or Valentine. Zina...how would she tell this story? It's in her voice, in my head, which is located in America now.

But my head was in her Odessa. When I waited in the airport to fly away, to fly home, I pictured Odessa from above. As my mind flew away, my body soon followed. My Russian is still fluent. It's not fluent enough to tell this story in Russian, though. It's enough to speak with my inner Zina. I drive around the destroyed landscape here in Detroit. It means nothing to me now. I want to see it from above. I want my inner Zina to fly me away from here on her silver tongue.

Her tongue I tasted. It was *spicy* like Odessan chestnuts, as Odessan as the wisps of grassy seaside air. I loved her tongue.

So now I should no longer speak Russian? There are two sides to every story. The real story comes out of what's least expected, what's not quite right. I'm an American, born and raised. This story made me foreign here in America. I'm here now on the opposite side of it, the opposite end from the day it began, even though it began here. But here wasn't here then. It was different. I loved Zina's tongue, and I want to become it. I want to spread my Odessan bird-of-paradise wings and fly like Zina did when she told stories.

7

Zina would think I stole her story and flew from Odessa with it. Sometimes I hear her tongue deep within my ear, a little Zina in a foreigner's mind.

Her father, Oleg, was convinced that America, where I am now, stole her away from him long before he even met me.

ONE

OLEG

I n February 2014, on the morning of the day when Zina would return to her motherland for the first time since leaving for America, Oleg's feet touched the floor early. Black tea finished the job of waking him. Half of a pan-warmed sausage and buckwheat kasha finished the job of feeding him. He was a freelance handyman and mechanic who specialized in maritime vehicles. He used to find jobs in the port. Now he typed inquiries into internet search engines. Either way, he still found next to nothing. He lived off next to nothing.

Now that Zina was returning home, he would need more, at least more than black tea, half a sausage, and kasha, even if it was buckwheat. The temperature in Celsius was already approaching *twelve*. To swim, his magic number was *fifteen*. He did a set of stretches for his knee to coax three more degrees of warmth from his motherland. He limped through the apartment littered with books piled alongside tiles, parquets, boxes of nails, a sander and behind a ladder draped with a sheet of canvas, the only occupants of his home since Zina left.

Outside the apartment, he could and did make wider strides. He had always annoyed his mother when he talked to himself. Then he annoyed Galka. Then Zina. *Snails for dinner. Probably, like an American, Zinochka will be sickened by snails.*

Down a crumbling path to Lanzheron Beach, he passed an acacia tree. He thought of the tiny yellow leaves that would be there in a couple months, how they would spiral slowly downward. The sky was clear, as was the beach, the water. He undressed, revealing beneath his shirt the chain from which hung a piece of shrapnel that had once occupied space inside his leg. *I'm that handy*, he would say if somebody asked where the shrapnel came from. He annoyed those who knew him, other *"specialists"*, with such talk.

If somebody asked, *Who swims in the Black Sea in February?* somebody else, somebody who knew Oleg, would answer, *He can take it.*

He wedged his feet into fins, grabbed his mask and snorkel, and made a splash as the water took him in. He plunged in the direction of the sea wall. After surfacing, he tried to float on his back, but his torso floated downward. In his mask, sky to sea to sky again. He snorted, sprayed water, flipped on his stomach, but still floated downward. A wave washed over his face. He took it and cleared his nostrils of the salty spray. There was no one in the water by any of the beaches stretching north to the city center or south past Ibitsa Beach, where the nightclub raged till morning. He dove, snatched snails from their paths along the silent floor.

Mackerel swam alongside the sea wall. He tried to mimic their languor. The anecdote went that, on the beach side of the sea wall, they waited for some fishing pole to snatch them from their lonely life. He had considered catching and releasing them into the wide world on the other side. He climbed and walked along the barnacled top. He dove and scooped several snails, placed them in the bag and, when it was full, twisted it shut and looped it around his wrist. *The job is such.* The *"Amerikanka,"* as he referred to his daughter, *should help save the sea. Eat snails—save the sea.*

Having almost filled his first bag, he surfaced and set it on the sea wall. His movements made the empty second bag billow with water. His mask fogged. That fog and the water lapping against the concrete and the waves along the sandy places took his memories. He used to swim out so far that the land was a fogged essence, against which the waves lapped and over which they washed until it was gone. He returned toward that essence, emerged, crossed the beach, and lay under a tree against the cliff over Lanzheron. On this sandy flat place he had lain, with a backpack for a pillow, so many drunken nights of his life. He remembered that morning every day. When he woke, Galka lay in bed with one eye open, her arm poised to push herself up. He dressed, came here to the beach. When he returned, his woman was gone. It was simple, a little bit stupid even. The man who came to collect Galka's bare essentials was quiet. And Oleg was glad for that. Zina was not quiet. *How could mama leave?*

Back then he was no good at thinking of anecdotes, so he simply answered, *How could mama arrive?*

Zina's arrival would be in a few hours, so he had to push himself up, take his backpack full of snails home, and sit on a bus to the Odessa airport.

An older man named Volodya was on the bus with Oleg. When Oleg was a boy, Volodya had taken him to weight lifting sessions. Now Volodya was complicated, like the intricate mechanisms he invited Oleg to fix at Volodya's dacha in Arkadia. Volodya couldn't use his own arthritic fingers. He asked, *Who in your family emigrated? Who's coming home?* The first of these questions had bothered Oleg most of all in his life. It was a light bother, like a stomach groaning. Yes, both his wife and his daughter had left Odessa behind. Lots of people leave their homes. And lots of people don't speak to their parents for lots of different periods of time.

Out of all that bother, an anecdote had arrived to him, and he answered Volodya with:

A boy and a girl lived in the same building where, without the supervision of their mamas, they played together when they were bored. The girl became sad often, counting the dark clouds. The boy took a toy airplane and scraped the air next to the girl's ear. "It's cleaning your bad thoughts away," the boy said. Whenever an airplane flew overhead, he said it was carrying away the girl's sadness. It seemed the boy knew by heart and could recite the schedule of the few airplanes that flew over their apartment because, as he declared this, one roared overhead. Maybe because it was so amazing for a little Odessitka, it worked. The girl became...happy.

At age sixteen, the girl's hand flew into the boy's when they met. At seventeen, they played tails and holes in the boy's room shared with his mama who was away, of course.

At eighteen, the boy went to say, "At your service!" in the Flot. The girl worried that something might pummel the voice out of his body. The girl put his words about her thoughts into the cabinet where they would sit alongside the beautiful dishes only to be used on special occasions, which became rarer and rarer until there were no more special occasions whatsoever. She looked at a knot in the cabinet which resembled a heart like the one in anatomy class. She didn't want the boy to see her cry. Boys didn't cry. Girls shouldn't either. But the girl wasn't an idiot. She knew the boy would know about how she put his words away, would know she cried. It was as if the boy lied about how he took away her sadness. It was as if he replaced it with a new sadness. There were more airplanes by this time. But now they brought sadness rather than carried it away. She watched them scrape the sky and wanted them to fall like flies. She swore always to remember this offense in her heart, which hurt and hurt until it became wooden.

When the boy returned from the Navy, he was wounded and, maybe for that reason, he wanted to wound others. He banged his fist into his palm. There were things he didn't tell the girl, things he might still want to do. He forgot how they walked in the forest nearby.

The girl waited. She gave birth to a baby. But she was still a girl who was waiting and waiting. While she waited, she liked to sip vodka in order to fly.

When the girl was a mama for seven years, she disappeared, leaving the boy and their daughter behind. She forsook where she came from. The boy and girl became two strangers. Neither of them told anybody their story. It felt unfinished, without an *ending, a kettle that screamed and was abruptly removed from the stove.*

What about the daughter? asked Volodya.
The daughter, well…
I can tell you wrote that down. That's unlike any anecdote I ever heard, Volodya said. *They say "Smells like an anecdote." That doesn't. And besides, anecdotes are usually a Jewish thing. About that Abramovich fellow.*
Well…, Oleg responded. He never finished his sentence, like so many didn't finish sentences during that uncertain time. Oleg didn't care if it smelled right. What good would it do to tell, instead of his anecdote, that his wife, the girl, left him because of a very small argument that took place in their kitchen and then echoed through his thoughts in the bathroom? He, the boy, charred some blintzes. Not long before, his wife read a book that said char caused cancer. It was an American book, poorly translated into Russian. In the bathroom, he swore to himself that he would separate with her. So it began. If they couldn't be in the kitchen without an argument, that meant it was the end because the kitchen is truly the home's heart. Then came that morning. *How could mama leave?*
Volodya limped out of the bus at a stop before they arrived at the airport. When Oleg, a bit more neatly, limped off, he realized that it was the second time in his life that he had been to the Odessa airport. He had studied the science of partings many times at the Odessa train station, closer to the center of the city. He had even thought of exiting the country he had known all his life. By the time glasnost had begun, the borders had opened up. The Berlin wall had come down. The country had locked down. *Maybe you won't be able to return,* his mother had said on the brink of her death, withering whatever bodily link with Soviet sentimentality existed. The TV had showed only *Swan Lake* on repeat, and the world of all Soviet people changed forever more. That

had been twenty-four years ago. During that time, a postcard had arrived from America, San Francisco to be precise, something he had never told Zina. Galka had become only a thread of correspondence, an abstraction, out there in the world. Packages of sweets and riches from San Francisco had arrived too. He wouldn't touch them with his finger, not to mention his tongue, and he had discarded them before Zina could see.

The only other time he had been to the Odessa airport was when Zina left on an airplane for America. While Zina was there, he would demand that she call him no matter the cost. He worried that something would be lost of their language, which meant their togetherness. It had been such a foolish reason for her to travel to America. Why find her mother, Galka, when Zina had Odessa, her motherland?

In truth, he had tried to live as if Galka never existed, had never been born nor, more to the matter, given birth. It was easy, the same way he lived with regard to his own father. Why did Zina need so much motherly love when he had been fine without a father?

Oleg loved to recite a true anecdote, not written by him, about delinquent dads. The punchline goes, *It's called immaculate conception.* Another one goes, *Abramovich complains to a stranger that he has no children. "It was the same with my father, and my grandfather too." With surprise, the stranger snorts, "Then where are you from?" "Odessa," Abramovich answers.*

And then there she was before him in the airport, as if she had been born of the Heavens. His dear daughter had returned. And there was an American with her.

TWO

ZINA, ZINKA, OR ZINOCHKA

Zina hissed, "The guide for tourists says *privyet* or *den dobryi* for hello. Not what I like to say, *drassss!* Anecdote." She switched to Russian with another heavy D sound. *Two travelers are on a boat. One asks, "Where are we headed?" "Yalta," says the other. The first says, "You said we're headed to Yalta because you thought I would*

think we're not headed to Yalta. But we're definitely headed to Yalta. Why are you lying?"

I didn't understand, Valinka said. So he switched. "I was just reading about this word, *tovarishch*, comrade. It's from Turkish. It's a commercial word. Capitalist."

Talkative, with more questions than answers, Valinka was womanly. Was that why Zina wanted him to come with her to Odessa? She looked through the glass wall of the Detroit airport, in the vacuum of which they sat. The wind had mutely twisted all the pieces of the world. She was returning home not with her mother, Galya, not even with a mother figure, and not even with a woman, but with a womanly person, at least.

On the walls were photographs of a Detroit-born *Great Patriotic War* sailor. She supposed the sailor himself would call it World War II. He had been lost at sea for three days. "My papa, he was in the Navy. You gonna meet him soon. So you gonna hear one of his stories. He once climb all the way to the top of the mast." Her English sounded better than ever, she thought to herself. "He is on the cruiser. There is the antenna there. A little ladder. You saw it? So, he swear this is true story. He was so high that he see fighter jets. They were American. One of this jets come so low that the American pilot wave at my papa. My papa almost fell into the water. My mama never believed this story." Her papa always said, at least, that she never believed.

Another one came to her. "Also, once, they catch the shark. They pull the shark onto the...*palubu*," her native language was regaining territory in her brain, "...and the shark, she is still alive. In Russian, *akula*. She. They caught her on the hook on the fucking chain." She could see other Americans nearby taking notice of her. She was loud, she was on her way out, thank God. "She jumping on the deck. The sailors cursing her. All she can do, she can growl. She growling at them. One sailor, one man, he put his fist in her eye." With her fist, Zina waved. "You know what she does? She jump and she eat his fucking arm off." The man next to them dropped his cell phone when Zina mentioned the bitten off arm. He and a woman next to him began to gather their items. "One bite." Zina laughed. The couple stood. While laughing, Zina saw the landscape again and longed to be able to sit and look out the window. "Point is, that like Ukraina. Don't fuck with her."

Valinka sat back and made a small tent with his fingers. He looked inside. In one of the spaces vacated by the Americans, she rested her feet. Now she had a better view of that mute, windswept world, which she could again witness. "Better than TV," she said. On the tarmac, the controllers were walking around with their glowing wands. Strolling was a better word for the way they walked. She wondered how much these jobs paid. They should pay well. Think of how much is involved, the responsibility of bringing these whales of the sky to the right place the right way, to tame them.

Valinka had taken out his Russian dictionary. She watched him flip the page, find the top corner of the next one. His eyes darted back and forth when he thought. Her papa's eyes did the same. She didn't know whether hers did.

She glanced out at the flat landscape of southeast Michigan, glared at how mute it was. The worst part of airports was the feeling of already being in soundless outer space. The wind was whipping the world, slapping surfaces and vibrating through metal sheets, shaking trees enough to shatter, and she could hear none of the destruction. "You read your books. But how you think it gonna be in Odessa? I guide you. But how you think it's gonna be?" she asked.

You should speak to me in Russian, was his answer.

On the tarmac, a controller, having fulfilled her duty for the time being, put her arms out Christ-like and fell into the wind, which held her for half a second before she stumbled and barely caught her upper body from slamming into the cement. Zina wished she could hear what kind of curses the woman was uttering. Maybe the controller wasn't cursing at all. She could be laughing. Other controllers approached her from a different side of the tarmac. One took her elbow in hand. They had a meeting there on the tarmac. One crouched down and began the arc of a slow-motion backflip, not completed. If Zina tried her hardest, she could imagine them speaking. The controller who had done the trust fall spoke Russian.

I'll tell you, she said, the way Galya would. It was time to speak the mother tongue. Upon hearing it, Valinka immediately put his dictionary away and sat upright. *The water around the port in Odessa is choppy with activity.*

We're flying in, he said.

Don't interrupt. I bought your ticket. You'll say, "There are the dachas of Odessa," when you see them. When we arrive, probably, it's red morning. As usual, there's a crowd when outsiders arrive. Odessa's in miniature, but it always feels as if it's in miniature. Watch out. There's a man in a peacoat, like the one I have from my papa. He'll greet you, request your passport. If you give it to him to hold, he'll walk away with it. He will shrug his shoulders the Odessan way as if he was a puppet, lifted for a moment by invisible strings hanging from the hand of God, who snatched him away with your passport. In short, don't give him your passport. Don't be swindled. He might have a little badge on a little chain. He might have a military uniform of some kind. Look around. There are many people with pieces of military uniform. This man has a fucking "budyonovka." What is it? It's what the Bolsheviks wore almost one hundred years ago. And this asshole wears a shirt with a loop of cloth for epaulets. No epaulets, though. This man wears several rings, clinking jewelry too large for hands that work on a ship. And in one of those hands is a cigarette. Don't speak a single word of English.

A young boy will remark on your beautiful shoes, unlike any he saw before in his life. A man with large cheek bones will size you up. Under the protruding Slavic bone of his cheek will be a scar. Everybody is still gaunt, as if it's still the nineties. If your passport was stolen, you'll find a policeman. You'll complain to him. He'll tell you, "Hello!" with a heavy KH sound. Then he'll say, "Follow me." Maybe he'll smile, but his voice won't. Your steps will echo along the cobblestones. When you complain again about your passport, he'll say, "Welcome to Odessa."

If you go to the police station, which I don't recommend, there will be a man without a uniform, in a suit instead. The suit doesn't fit him. How could a suit fit him? Even he's gaunt. When you complain, he'll raise his index finger to an evil smile. "Can you prove you're American another way?"

Another cop will say, "Ask him if he has any dollars to prove it." For them you are exotic, a trinket from America, a souvenir.

If not for me, this tragedy would happen. If not for me, you would stay in a hotel by the central port, where all the foreigners live. You would have a view of the stairs of Potemkin, the Opera Theater, small sailboats, high cliffs overlooking beaches, the walls of an aqueduct. It would cost a lot more money than you have, all your money for a long time.

I'll take care of you now. You'll live with me and my papa. You must speak Russian.

Imagine what it was like for a woman who came to your country.

This womanly person, whose eyes were glazing over, who was clearly not listening, this Valinka Zina was bringing to the place of her birth, the place where she lived most of her life, the place where, probably, she would die. She would not be able to return to the United States of America, the land where Galya was. Maybe she should go, at least, to where Galya was from? Not Poltava. Galya from Poltava, a Poltavka, came to Odessa, married an Odessan, learned Odessan anecdotes — many of them having to do with poor Abramovich — so well that the Poltavka became an honorary Odessitka. And she had herself a child Odessitka. Maybe now she was too much of an Amerikanka to be an Odessitka anymore.

The Odessitka needed to keep telling Valinka about Odessa. *This place was Kievskaya Rus, became the Russian Empire, became the Ukrainian Soviet Socialist Republic, and became Ukraine. Each place was an acacia petal, rising in the breeze, floating, only to fall underfoot*

19

*again. Like the tongue speaking Russian, it touches the top of the mouth
at times, for the soft sign, or to say the name of my birthplace properly:
Odyessa. "Odd Yes Ah." The breeze there carries the smell of grass and
sea. Those petals come to a rest on shellrock both gentle and strong. That
shellrock was unearthed to build that city on its own hollows, which run
all the way to Tairovsky Cemetery, one of the biggest in Ukraine. There,
they say, lies an entrance to the catacombs.* Galya, in her mind, said,
Sh, don't tell anybody about it.

Her anecdotes touched Valinka, unearthed him, and this power
made her an honorary Odessitka again. Ah Deceit Ka. He called
this Odessitka Zina, short for Zinaida, which nobody would have
called her. He could call her Zinka or Zinochka too if he wanted. If
he called her Zinaida, she would stick her tongue out in his face. If
that hurt his feelings, he might not stick it out in Odessa.

You were never an honorary Amerikanka, Galya said inside Zina.
Her American dream had begun twenty years ago when Zina was
seven, when she woke one morning to find that her mama left her
and papa and traveled to America. Now, slouching in the airport,
Zina could feel it coming to an end.

When Zina had asked why Mama left, her papa told her it
was because her mama had wanted a car, something which, in
Odessa, he had never possessed the means to acquire. When
Zina read the list of the cities in which Gastarb East — the guest
worker program that was her ticket to the USA — would offer em-
ployment, she picked the one where they made all the cars for all
the Americans. She picked the city of Detroit. Through Gastarb
East, a McDonald's near the Corktown neighborhood of Detroit
sponsored Zina to work. The American dream was ready for her,
the same way it had laid itself prostrate before her mama. Her
mama, though, had a man. Zina was alone. The closest she had
to a man had been a Ukrainian-American in the Detroit area. He
had friended her on ibook.com. His name was Valentine Pech-
enko, and he had offered a space where she could live. He was

a self-proclaimed Socialist and lived in what he thought was a communal apartment. He was even learning Russian. It was a start, a communal apartment. The next step would be her very own room. The American dream was one's own apartment. Her mama probably shared one with her man. The American dream was what had brought her mama to America. If Zina stayed in America too, her papa would die. The American dream was, therefore, the dream of the Western enemy, who wanted to kill a poor old Soviet.

When Zina had arrived here, she had passed through Customs more easily than when she had left Ukraine, where she had been asked several times whether she was a prostitute. Now she expected it would be easier on the Ukrainian side.

When she had arrived here, she had taken a bus from the airport into the city. The bus heaved through regions of the Detroit metropolitan area that resembled the industrial outskirts of Odessa. It was a translation. The towers built outside the city center of Odessa had their translations here too. Neither kind of structure was a place to live. It was a place to put people until they died. It was not a dwelling. It was housing. In Detroit, there were individual bricks. In Odessa there was more lightly colored cement, a broad seamless swath.

She had thought she could translate the dream back into something she and her mama spoke in Odessa. The American dream became the American joke.

In Detroit, Zina had exited the bus, walked, and finally dropped her duffel bag on a patch of sidewalk at the intersection of two streets. Inside were her clothes, a notepad, and her items of hygiene. Along these streets ran empty dirt fields, lots with cement paths leading to nothing. There must have been homes here once. Zina had wondered where all those people migrated, where their dreams had taken them and from which dirty bus station they had departed. A rhythmic drilling had been audible there, although it was unclear from which side it was coming or whether it came from the ground itself. To this emptiness and its drilling, which was as black and without echo as the hinterland between Odessa and Kiev, she said, *Greetings*. Her papa had taught her this word. It was one of the first learned in Russian. Many learners, like this Valentine she was about to meet, couldn't even make it past those three initial consonants, *Zdr*. Once somebody could say *Greetings* without thought of the drilled suddenness of the sound, they were on their way to familiarity with the listener.

The sound was too omnipresent to hear the car which had turned at the end of one axis of the emptiness and now trolled toward her. When it pulled up alongside, the back door opened. A human coat hanger, who must have been Valentine, stepped out. Zina herself was gaunt. Odessans who had traveled to America had told her that Americans were all fat. If that was the case, Valentine was truly not an American. Only his baggy clothing made him appear as if, like a blowfish, he was prepared to become fat — that is, to become American — in an instant. Out of his pocket, he took a pack of cigarillos. She had seen such before, never smoked one. In his email, he had explained in misspelled Russian that he was a socialist. What kind of a socialist smokes cigarillos? Socialists smoke cigarettes. He lit up and took a drag from the cigarillo, put out his hand, and took one step toward her. He mispronounced, *"Zdravstvuite,"* as if in much delayed response to the greeting she had cast over the emptiness before he arrived.

The dream had been strong and brave and had seized her heart then. She had asked Valentine why his family had come here. After stubbing out his cigarillo, he said, *My father...he's from Odessa. He didn't like Odessa. So he left. He didn't like Detroit either.* Odessan humor sounded like it was in Valentine's blood even though he had never been there. The other side of it was, of course, that he left Detroit too, left Valentine and his mother. Zina knew about parents leaving. Back then she believed that Valentine would understand the joke about Yalta, about how the one traveler expects something more than what the other traveler says, expects two different, contradictory messages, they're going to Yalta, which means they might not be going to Yalta, which means they're definitely going to Yalta. That was what she thought back then.

Valentine asked if she spoke and read Ukrainian. She said she spoke and read Ukrainian, Russian, and, most of all, Odessan, the language of those anecdotes. He asked, *Should I say "in" Ukraine or "on" Ukraine?*

"Say Odessa. I am from Odessa," she told him. He did so, and then he took her to his "home."

THREE

I, Valinka

n the apartment where Zina and I lived, broken pieces of various items lay scattered across the floor. A banshee's bad breath stagnated in the mute space. Clothes, notebooks of lyrics, brimming ash trays, tools, and our landlord's guitar all lay around in a way that made it obvious Zina had picked each item up, turned it over in her hands mindlessly for a while, dropped it, and herself flopped down alongside. The sink contained an architecture of dirty dishes, neglect, and time.

The landlord, Linda, never addressed the lack of tidiness and never addressed me at all. She would come over, and the two of them, Zina and Linda, would sit there giggling. When I would ask a question, they'd answer as succinctly as possible and start giggling again. Otherwise, silence. Finally, I'd leave them alone. I understood. They were fucking. For whatever reason, they kept it from me. That hurt. The language was what connected us. Linda couldn't speak Russian. I spoke better Spanish than Zina, and my Spanish is shit. At least I had that on Zina: her Spanish was shittier than mine.

Outside, despite the perpetual fart smell, the grass glistened with a toxic magic, tiny particles of hot metal which had rained from the clouds issued by the refinery on the end of the spanning industrial block. *Is this like the dangerous landscapes of the former Soviet Union?* I once asked Zina while Linda snored. She said, "Not Odessa."

"*Odyessa, Odyessa,*" I would repeat to myself the way she said it. A steel structure over the road where we lived read AbANdON ALL HOpE. Linda always pointed it out, even after we had passed underneath several times. Yet each time Zina gave a little chuckle and shook her head at me.

In those notebooks I found notes from Linda: "I know this ain't gonna last. But you better not ever forget me. Suka." Linda had learned the Russian word for *bitch*. "You're going to be obsessed with me. You started with me. You can't unring a bell. You're going to wish you never met me for what I do to you. Yesterday when you kissed my fat rolls, my lips, tried to speak Spanish right into my pussy. I felt like you were trying to go inside me, inside my skin. Remember when we learned that word 'tribbing.' Then we did it? I put a spell on you then. In Spanish so you couldn't understand. You'll start to dress like me, act like me. You'll slowly turn into me. When you look in the mirror, when you see the way

25

others, the sukas, look at you, you'll see me, deep inside." And Zina's lyrics: *My love's a depraved slave/ She'll do whatever you want, you're warned/ She's old, knows too much/ She'll let you down.* Of course she'd written them for Linda. However, they were in Russian, so I couldn't help from putting myself into the *you* of them.

Then I found the video they made. Zina smiles into the camera. She goes down on Linda, lying reclined. Linda says, "Soy bruja," which I know means *I'm a witch*, like something from Zina's lyrics, "*Ya vedma.*" Then Linda says some Spanish words which I don't understand. Her moans become louder. She closes her eyes. Zina moves toward Linda and sits in her lap. They roll onto their sides and begin to scissor. Zina looks back into the camera. Her eyes flare. She says, *You're home?* Or she could have said *house.* Linda sits up, says, "I don't speak Russian," pushes Zina away, and grabs the phone to switch off the video.

Days later, while we were drinking, I used my elementary school Spanish and put the word *casa* out there, as if I had read it off some text, as if it had fallen into my lap. "It means *home.* Or *house*," I said.

Zina flared up, said, "All the people, who they speak better English me. They don't do nothing with their lives. They just speak the better English me." She waited to make sure I'd heard. "Like you, Valinka. What you do?"

I took the bottle from her. *I speak Russian. That's what I do*, I said.

Zina gave a tiny chuckle. "Yeah? You speak Russian? You nothing but the Russian speaker? What are you, Valinka? Nobody knows."

Linda doesn't speak Russian, I pleaded.

That night she retreated to the bathroom with Linda's guitar. She played a dark fast rhythm and sang the way a cornered dog would. There was a grinding scrape. I knocked, waited, knocked again, and finally said, *All good?* I heard panting. I used my thumbnail to undo the lock.

She was on the floor, naked, yanking the strings of Linda's guitar, wrenching them so hard that the high E and B strings had come loose and pricked her, drawing blood. I said nothing, watching her mutilate the guitar and her forearm. Her blood dribbled and was smeared over the white of the linoleum. She took the high string and tied it around her wrist. It was intentional, of course, although I didn't really understand how it could be dangerous. *Don't*, I said. I stopped because I couldn't think of the word for suicide. All that was left was that phrase, hanging in the air, "*Ne nado.*"

"What?" She saw her own nakedness and gasped when she saw that I was witnessing it too. She yanked a towel off the rack. "What you fucking say to me? What words you say to me? You know what this words, this Russian words, mean? You know what they mean?" I tried to answer her questions. She continued over my volume. "Fuck you. Speak English. You can't speak fucking Russian, fucking idiot. You fuck up Russian."

I decided to relent. I had succeeded in talking her down from suicide in her own language. "Sorry for trying to stop you from committing suicide," I said with irony. "I love you," I said.

I think she gave up on what brought her to America, her mom, that night.

And she admitted to nothing. "You think I kill myself with the fucking guitar string?" She looked at her own wrist. "I just think it is pretty." She rubbed it on her face and cooed, "Mamochka." She kicked at the door, and it slammed shut the second I backed out of the way.

She spent the night in there and had cleaned up her gore by morning and never mentioned it again.

My hope was that, if not sooner, by the time we reached Ukraine, Zina would start to speak Russian with me.

The morning Zina and I left for Odessa, she wore heels for the first time in this country. She had stolen them from Linda. I followed behind as she clacked down the street toward the bus stop in the direction of the airport. We were leaving our cozy little apartment with its garbage and lassitude. My life in the English-speaking world was coming to an end. All Zina had was me, her Valinka. Nobody in Ukraine could tell the part that happened in English. Nobody here can tell the part that happened in Russian, Odessan Russian. My English and my Russian are all this story has.

When the bus arrived, the driver slowed, took a look at us, and gunned it—as much as a bus could gun it. I could swear I saw him mouth, "Fucking foreigners." Even though she could afford it, I knew Zina wouldn't want to pay for a cab to the airport from all the way in Mexicantown Detroit. We both turned and began to walk toward the freeway.

Within minutes we were climbing an onramp. *You know this is illegal*, I said.

"That I am in America is illegal now," Zina responded.

We strode along the freeway for about ten minutes. There was only the distant whir of an airplane engine. It was early enough that the sun was still rising, burning through the clouds to brighten the littered freeway, the cool breeze drawing some of the exhaust out of the air we breathed. Everything hummed. We were beginning to freeze.

A cab driving in the other direction slowed, cut across a couple lanes, ground over the meridian. The cab zoomed across to the shoulder where we stood. Zina said, "We close enough now," and waved.

The cab pulled closer to us, and the driver asked from his window, "Airport?" Zina nodded for us both. He popped the trunk, and I put Zina's suitcase and my backpack inside. We sat in the cab, again on our way to Ukraine by vehicle rather than by foot.

Day brightened the sky over the Michigan treeline. I decided to make one last phone call, even if only to my father's voicemail, before I shut my cell phone off for what could have been forever.

Hearing the Russian I had spoken for this voicemail, the driver said, "I am from Kharkov. Where you go?"

"Odessa, Ukraine."

"Odessa is not the *Ukraina*," the driver said as he veered and corrected. He'd glanced at himself in the side mirror when he pronounced the name of his country. Now he shifted to see me in the rearview. "You Jew?"

"*Nyet*," I said.

"You don't got no family there? They gonna have good time with you," he said. The laughter began in his gut and sounded as if it were coming from a place very far away, very deep inside the man's grizzled, bristly jowls and rolls of fat.

The sun was bright enough now that each of us squinted. The airport tower loomed beyond glinting barbed wire fences. The smell of exhaust filled the cab. I slipped my hand into my pocket and pressed my passport. When I turned eighteen, my father had said, "A man needs a passport. You know how valuable is an American passport?"

I was trying to remember Russian words, overthinking what I would say to the driver. How would I be able to live when I couldn't even tell a joke in Russian? "'Cause you can't speak Russian," my father had said. The driver opened his window. Zina turned her head to avoid the gust.

Before I followed Zina out of the cab, the driver rasped, "Have nice trip." After I shut the trunk, the cab sped off, making a drunken swerve to avoid a pedestrian.

"We should support civil liberties and opt out of the X-ray scan at security," I mentioned off-handedly to Zina. She gaped at me like a newborn bird.

At security, studying the floor, I forgot about opting out. When Zina asked about it, the TSA agents rolled their eyes. Fucking foreigners. I kept my mouth shut, so they would think I was a fucking foreigner too.

Zina didn't have any trouble with leaving since she was doing a "voluntary departure." We sat by the gate and waited. I took out my Russian dictionary and continued reading. I was going through it word-by-word. I was in the Ls. Their burden weighed on my tongue. I thought it was because it was burdened by the Russian *Ls*. English Ls in Cyrillic are always followed by the *soft sign*. I had first learned the Russian *L* sound when I'd been speaking words out of the dictionary earlier, when I was in the Vs. When I spoke out loud the Russian word for wolf, Zina demanded I repeat several times. "It is not 'folk.'" Even after I said the Russian word for wolf several times, my American tongue still couldn't bow down enough for it. Russian Ls were not *soft*. My tongue needed to lift weight.

Realizing I had passed over several words unconsciously, I dropped the dictionary face-down in my lap. Our neighbor announced to the man sitting next to her, "I'm going to find a bathroom."

"All right," the man said without looking up from his phone.

Upon return from the bathroom, she said, "Touchdown."

"Touchdown," the man said, giving a quick smile without turning from his phone.

Eventually, Zina scared these people away. She almost scared me away. Once we got in line, she dodged people in order to get ahead, maybe in order to avoid me. I wondered what would happen when we landed. Would she simply run away, leave me at the airport? That didn't sound like her since she had bought the tickets with money her father had wired her from Ukraine.

At Trumbulldome, the commune where I lived when I first met Zina, my friend Lionel once said that people must put their affairs in order before traveling. It may be the last time a person stands on his native soil, even on this plane of existence.

Standing on the thin, industrial carpeting of the airport before we boarded, I wondered whether I should keep a diary in Odessa. I thought I had put all my affairs in order except for those between my father and myself. He left Odessa when he was thirty-seven years old. Would switching sides make me better? I asked myself whether he spoke English better when he left than I spoke Russian now, at twenty-five, the age of my self-imposed exile. If I ever returned, my Russian would be good enough that he would have to speak with me in his native language.

A suitcase handle poked my butt. A nervous sigh warmed the back of my head. I turned, and the holder of the suitcase, the sigher, stepped once-and-a-half to run into me again. Although I moved forward to soften the collision, I could only take one step. Behind me I heard Russian cursing. I heard, "*Do svidaniya.*" Of course, I knew this means *Until next time.* I imagined these words spoken in my father's Russian voice, which I'd almost never heard. He was saying goodbye to me in the end.

My neighbor on the airplane was a man the same age as my father. He flapped his newspaper and, from the corner of his eye, noticed my dictionary. He mumbled something. *What?* I said.

In English, the man said, "You read Russian?"

I try. I'm Ukrainian.

"Don't try to speak Russian. Better speak to me in English."

But I'm Ukrainian. I'm American but with Ukrainian roots.

"Yes, I got it. You are Ukrainian."

My father is Ukrainian. My mother's American.

"What does it mean he is Ukrainian? Many people say that, but he is from Russia."

My father's from Odessa, which, allegedly, isn't Ukraine.

"The Ukraine has different sides. East and South are Russified. West is very different. Catholic. This is current problem."

I know.

The man laughed. "You travel much to Odessa?"

No. This is my first time.

"You have family there?"

No.

"Your father?"

What about him. The tone had not been that of a question.

"I only ask, friend. You seem like good boy. Watch out when you are in the Ukraine. Things are happening there. It will be bad. It will make you bad."

I refrained from commenting on the use of the article before Ukraine. "My father left when he was thirty-seven. Never been back. He's very stubborn, Americanized, I guess. I'm trying to, sort of, reclaim my heritage. I want to be able to speak the language my ancestors spoke." The airplane had started to move. The man said something in Russian again. I didn't care because I had responded to him. I had overcome his challenge. I wasn't afraid. I nodded. Still, the lack of understanding wounded me. The sound, meaningless to me, was unforgettable.

I grow. Russian words fill wounds like this. Scar tissue closes around them. The time will come in this story when I will know the Russian word by the time I reach the end of the paragraph. The next stage will be when, by the time the period stops the very same sentence, I'll have resolved understanding of any words lingering in my ear.

FOUR

ZINA

When the land of Zina's birth was rushing to meet the wheels of the airplane, her mind filled with white noise. When the airplane had touched down and stopped taxiing, she heard a wail from some passenger's headphones. She pressed closer to the window. The door would open, the prodigal child would return. She could hear her papa's shuffle. She had to prepare herself for his tiny coughs, the awkward rise and fall of his voice as he ticked off the problems of America against the pleasures of Odessa. She had to prepare to laugh off his impotent anger, how he would grit his teeth and make his mouth a flat line, a worm trying to hurry away in a huff.

During the descent, she had seen a backyard with white dots scurrying. The dots were chickens, goose-stepping like the Red Army on parade, little legs like the bars of a typewriter. In Detroit, chickens had marched in the backyard of Trumbulldome. The place resembled a village church, three stories climbing heavenward, surrounded by chickens at its base. It even had an onion-shaped dome.

Valentine had called "home" a *kommunalka*. It was an old mansion that groaned and smelled of kerosene. All that was left of the carpets were roughly cut fringes along the baseboard. Doors and hinges were removed from the cabinets, knobs from the doors. The other residents — Brittney, Haley, and Roberto — welcomed Zina as if she had already lived there for months, maybe a year. "Hello," they said. "Cool," instead of nice to meet you. She followed Valentine up the stairs. When they reached the top and made turns as if down the halls of a communal apartment building from the Soviet era, she said, *like home*, and Valentine stopped, turned back to her, and grinned. What she did not do in response caused him to bow and stare at the floor. After this moment of reverence to the house, they entered a room, and he shut the door behind himself. Zina immediately understood that what Valentine had meant as a space in a room, commune-style, was really a space in a room with only one bed. What he had meant by a space was a floor, a space that, normally, people walked on.

The fifty dollars a month will go to my friend Ben, whose room this is. He speaks Russian.

You're serious? Zina backed up from him and bowed. "This is not space in room. This is not worth shit."

"Okay," he said. At first, the American shrugged like an Odessan operator, like he didn't care what her needs were.

"I trust you about your space," she said.

Care filled his features. He looked at her as if for the first time. "Okay. You don't have to pay anything." All of a sudden, he was unlike an Odessan operator.

"Why you say this? You lie?" She was here. He had what he wanted. Now he would attack. She bent at the knees, balled her fists.

"No. I didn't lie. I don't pay anything either. Sorry. My Russian's not very good."

"*Nyet*," she said. She dropped her duffel bag. Bring the opponent closer to you, she had learned in *SAMBO*, self defense. She was ready, decidedly ready, to kill him for the wrong move.

"I'm sorry," he said. His English didn't affect her. He said, *Excuse me*.

"You were wrong," she said. "Say this."

"I was wrong," he said. "How do I say it in Russian?"

"I have no time to find other place. You are sorry?" she asked. He nodded and looked at her again, now clearly caring whether she would leave. *An anecdote*, she began. *Abramovich offended his friend.* "What do you want me to say?" he asked the friend. The friend said, "Say, 'I was wrong. You were right. I'm sorry.'" Abramovich said, "I was wrong? You were right? I'm sorry." Valentine's bafflement was real. She had needed to explain that it was all about the inflection. Instead of statements, the would-be guilty party said, "I was wrong? You were right?" and only said, "I'm sorry," as a kind of polite dismissal of the very idea that he could be wrong and Abramovich right.

Now, in Odessa, it was her turn to play hostess. Now his bafflement would not only be real, it would be constant.

How horrible you look, her papa said, grinning to soften his words. It was true. She was pale and skinny, more like a boy than a woman. She had thought she was going to cry. Seeing the dry

35

land of Ukraine hardened her, for the time being. *I thought you would never return*, he said. On the airplane, a young girl had said in Russian, *The bigger the raindrop, the faster it falls.*

She had not brought Valinka to Odessa to baffle him. His presence, even in some unknown seat on the airplane, like that of a stowaway in her life, saved her. She remembered when she first caught glimpse of his mind, what it was like inside of that skull with dark, wavy locks. In that room that first day in Detroit, there had been a desk. On that desk was a notebook. Its proximity to her, once she had sat down, made him do a little pout. It was something of value to him. She opened it, watched from the corner of her eye for what he would do, and read: "Failure has power." She stopped, looked at him. These words matched the failure of his outfit. "For decades the Revolution failed. Failed in England. Failed in Germany. But the Revolution happened in Russia, a country at the time more like rural Michigan than industrial Detroit." She believed he was what he appeared and sounded to be. She read further while he grunted and shifted. "Failure whittled the Russian people down to those sharp enough for the Revolution. Failure, losing, these things make a Revolutionary better hear the tones of the Revolution. It's better not to hear the chimes of happiness, prosperity." In smaller, shrewder letters, he wrote: "My father, whom I will now only refer to by his name, Anatole...Anatole couldn't handle that country. Nor could he handle Michigan, Detroit. He escaped the Revolution. He's an enemy of it...her. *Revolutsiya* is a feminine word. *Ona*." He wrote *she* instead of it. The only women who gave him the time of day were ideologies, bodiless, like the smoky woman on his pack of cigarillos. From the shelf above the desk, Valentine had taken a tome by Marx in order to give the appearance that he himself was reading and not paying attention to her reading his diary. In some ways, she felt like she was reading the American version of her own diary. His papa had not liked Detroit. Her mama had not liked Odessa, had not liked Ukraine. To herself she recited the punchline to another anecdote about the Odessan named Abramovich. She knew so many anecdotes about Abramovich, all of which her papa and her mama had demanded she memorize. The punchline went, *All that's left of my father is my patronymic.* It was utterly untranslatable. Valentine, at least, would understand. She saw that he wrote, "The Revolution's my mother, Russian my father." And Ukraine's my crazy aunt, she wanted to add.

Ukraine, namely Odessa, had nonetheless drawn her home. Here in Odessa, she fell asleep in the backseat of an unmarked taxi and woke to the door opening with a sucking sound resembling that of a kiss, like those Galya gave when Zina was still Galya's daughter. When Galya was still Zina's mama, Galya would come and kiss her ear. This gush of sound had woken her so many times. This time such a kiss was unreal. It had been a dream of a sound. Galya had approached her in this dream and left a kiss at the opening of her ear. It was a farewell. Or the sound had been her own tongue, which flailed in her dry mouth now. After America, where Galya remained, Zina's tongue was an exhausted seahorse. Now America was nothing more than a word.

Once she had asked her mama how she became so smart. *Years of loneliness*, Mama had said. After allowing several long seconds of dead silence to pass, Mama had begun to laugh. She had laughed so deeply that Zina could see all the way to the punching bag inside Mama's throat. Mama had been a monster with a gaping mouth. Maybe Mama's years in America had softened her. Maybe she would have wanted to return to her hard ways if Zina had found her.

When she had asked Valentine about the bathroom, he had lead her back downstairs and outside. At the opposite end of the backyard was a makeshift outhouse, within which was a pit with two-by-fours set in a square on the brim. Next to it was a bucket of ash. A hose on a hook was the sink. There was even a sign stating that everybody should sit, since the collective's rules demanded equity between genders. Valentine had to sit there too. Zina laughed. "This is like in motherland!" She told an anecdote: *Somebody asked Abramovich, "Why do you sit when you pee?" Abramovich answered, "Since childhood, I believed that my late forebears could see through my eyes that which I do." That somebody said, "I don't understand." Abramovich quickly answered, "You think I want them to see my privacy, my innermost?"* She watched Valentine and knew that he had not understood the joke. Even though Valentine understood Russian, he still had a long way to go to understand an Odessitka like her. Nonetheless, she had trusted him because he spoke Russian. She had trusted him because, in the country that demanded of all the world's inhabitants that they speak English, one was willing to speak her language. Now Valentine had provided her with a pillow and blanket, a pad to put underneath. She trusted him because, even in English, even on the first day they met, he had shown his innermost to her. She had lain down to sleep while he stayed up reading by the desk lamp. After some grunts and other puzzled sounds, he had switched the light off, clicked the doorknob, and lay down beside her. He never touched her, never crossed the whisper's distance between them.

Into that floor Valentine had carved the Cyrillic letters Ц, Ч, and У. Before Zina's mama left, she used to lie next to Zina in bed and trace the letters of the alphabet in random order on Zina's back. It was Zina's duty to guess correctly which letters she traced. Her mama taught Zina literacy this way. Often Zina would fall asleep during the process, not because the alphabet or literacy was boring but because of their mutual innermost, like a blanket around them.

In Detroit, that first night, sleep had come. She had not been able to sleep like those who live safe lives do. But it had come, had begun and lasted, and she had dreamed of the place where she was at that moment, that she was sleeping uncomfortably, that there were no sounds in the house where everybody was sleeping.

Now she slept that way on the first night of her return to Ukraine, to Odessa, to her papa's apartment.

She woke when she heard the jiggle of the doorknob. Yes, she was in Odessa again. Surrounding her were the objects of her papa's office. For example, there were grooves where her papa's body had been born by the seat of the aching chair. However, there were also items kept from her childhood, a box of toys. In it was a clown puppet on a stick. His name was Pierrot. For a clown, his face was sad. Pierrot the clown collapsed into a cone. As he collapsed, a wooden peg extended from the point of the cone. Holding the cone point down, Zina pushed the peg up, and the opposite happened. Pierrot's felt body rose and expanded. His arms opened as if to embrace everybody with his wan joy.

The toy had come from her papa's childhood, and she herself had played with it so much that it had begun to come loose at the base of the cone. As a small child, she had known that one day Pierrot would no longer be attached. So she stopped playing with him to put off the inevitable. She put it out of her head. Now she had returned to Pierrot and his soft, sliding felt sound. It was subtle. The peg pushed that grin out at the world. His arms draped alongside. Pierrot wasn't happy, wasn't sad, was merely the ball at the other end of the peg. He was like a souvenir for Odessa the way Valinka was the small piece of America which she had brought with her.

Valinka she had forgiven because he had inflected himself to her. In her primary language, questions were simply matters of inflection. Like with the *I'm wrong. — I'm wrong?* anecdote, there was the question, *You want something for this?*, like when she first saw the room. When Valentine took back his request, made eye contact with her, she could inflect the same words to make the statement, *You want something for this.* And that was not happy, not sad, but very small.

That first morning in Detroit, she had awoken to the pleasantly familiar, sad sound of a mourning dove, a bird with which she was very familiar because of her name, part of the Latin name for the *crying pigeon*, as mourning doves are called in Russian. The "Oooo-EE-ooo-oo-oo" sound came from outside Trumbulldome's rosette window through which the room filled with light. Without that light, she had not noticed the rosette window when she fell asleep. The window was massive, taking up almost the entire wall on the front of the house and, like a perversely large eye, ogling her. Valentine lay asleep, his hand resting across a tome, an English translation of Marx, as if across a teddy bear.

That tome he had checked out from the library, which she visited that first morning. After climbing some stairs, she entered a long room. When she turned around, she saw above the entrance a mural depicting a white man with arms out, Christ not fixed to any cross. Behind him rockets were launching. Zina thought of how, when they painted this mural, those rockets were likely launching into a trajectory toward her motherland. Instead of into Soviet murals, this mural translated, to her, into an anti-American poster her papa had kept from the late sixties, back in Odessa. There was a body depicted in that poster too, only the body was hanging from its neck while angels mounted a backwards American flag. The poster said, *And in your place, they're lynching Negroes!* Her associations were still stuck in the Cold War which had officially ended before she was five years old.

There were stairs made out of what looked like the same stone that made up almost all of Odessa, shellrock. One doorway through which she walked was so short that even she had to duck underneath. On a nearby shelf, Zina spotted Cyrillic and thought of how at least she had found her mother tongue if not her mama herself. She pulled the book and was immediately gentle. It was lighter than she anticipated. Its age must have caused it to shrink and dry out, become little more than dust, once stuck together by some fluid. Now it had only a barely adhering structure. She opened to a middle page. The book was pre-Soviet and still had the letter *yat*. It was the language of that dust. It was before the regime which had defined the lives of every generation she had known in her country. She put it away as if it were poison. Further down she found a nineteen thirties journal written by Russian-language anarchists and published here in Detroit. She leered at the journal, *Probuzhdenie*, while she thought about how her people were here before anybody in the room with her was born.

She listened to these people, Americans, speak. "What are you gonna do? Get a book?"

"Yeah, I'm gonna get a book."

"Then get it. I got shit to do, man. You're gonna miss out with these books."

She found a title she liked, a book called "Them" by Joyce Carol Oates. As she sat down to read, exhaustion washed over her like the noise of a jet engine. After reading only ten pages for an hour, she left the library and came around the block to Woodward Avenue. During that first twenty-four hours after arrival in America, when she had crossed Woodward on her way to Trumbulldome, she had thought the wide arterial street of Detroit was like the Odessan *Boulevard of the Big Fountain*. Some black girls said, "With that Elmer Fudd hat," about her plaid cap, given by her papa. She thought that she wanted to hate them. She next thought, *Did their father give them anything?* and the voice in her head thinned to a whimper as she looked down Woodward and gasped at the blank expanse. The wide street had also made her think of *Nevsky Prospekt* or of *Tverskaya*.

However, she had never been to St. Petersburg or Moscow. And now, back in Odessa, it felt as if she had never been to Detroit either.

FIVE

VALYA

The scientific name for the mourning dove is zenaida macroura. This fact is one I found out while trying to understand Zina, Zinaida, the strange avis who came into my life. She was always far from me. On both legs of the flight, we hadn't sat together. Zina had paid for our tickets. I hadn't been in a position to demand that she pay extra so we could choose our seats.

At one point, I had entered the airplane restroom and, when the door was stuck, stood there in the darkness. Zina had already felt out this place to which we were traveling. For me, it was small, too enclosed, like the restroom. I was used to the wide-open prairie that was once a city called Detroit.

When I had exited and sat down for the descent, I could see this kind of landscape below. Vast open spaces were marked by pieces of leftover industrial infrastructure. I'd come from one wasteland to another. The Odessa airport was the size of a large barn.

As we shuffled into that barn, I couldn't find Zina. Ahead of me, I heard only wicked laughter and the word *Amerikose*. Zina would say, That's too derogatory a word for an American like you, Valinka.

At Ukrainian Customs, the agent yawned, *Well, do you understand Russian?*

I nodded. *I don't speak Ukrainian.*

No? the agent replied in mock surprise. He began to yawn again. *I also don't speak Ukrainian. Why have you come?*

43

Tourism, I told him.

By the time he finished the second yawn, he'd stamped my passport. Around the corner was a gauntlet of people staring at me from the other side of a movable barrier. Their faces, their outstretched hands showed an eagerness to take me where I should be. I didn't know where I should be, so I walked as if with earmuffs and blinders.

There was Zina by a gaunter version of my father. It was as if my father had recently come from a funeral. He was speaking to her alone in such a way that it was clear Zina had neglected to mention me to him. I was lucky. She didn't embrace this man at first. She only sniffed. With yawning eyes she looked at him, leaned toward him, and kissed him on the cheek. I found myself glaring at her father. I inwardly demanded that he appreciate her kiss.

He wasn't paying any attention to me at all. He said, *I thought you'll never return*. He used the *tu*, as in you singular. Who was returning? Not I.

Zina let out a deep breath. *Papa, this is Valinka. He's my friend. He came to visit us in Odessa.* She watched him. His face hardened. *Acquainted? Valinka, here's my father, Oleg.* She picked up her bag and continued on her way past us.

He looked as if he was going to curse. Outside the window, a small airplane lurched past, Lufthansa written on the side. A man walked alongside, his jaw clenched, head bobbing to music from earphones. He wore a shirt that said "G-UNIT." Outside the sky was orange layers descending to the earth.

You're joking, he called to Zina. He hadn't been able to keep eye contact with me for long. When he looked at me again, he said, "Guten Tag. Sprechen Sie Deutsch?" This piqued G-UNIT's interest.

"Ja," I said. I had learned a little German in high school.

"*Amerikanets?*" he asked.

"Ja," I said. I didn't know what to say.

"Ich kann kein Englisch," Zina's father told me.

I speak Russian, I said while I let my hiker's backpack down. My clothes had pasted themselves to my clammy skin. I could feel the burden of what hung inside my clothing, my passport and wallet. Everything moved slowly, like the foot of a snail, simultaneously sticking to and peeling from the surface. *My papa is Odessan.*

This gaunt version of my father wore his shirt unbuttoned. His chest was exposed. The airport was warm, and he'd made himself comfortable during the long wait. His ropy arm slung out and snatched my backpack. Outside, the airplane sat, waiting to return, I suppose, to where I'm writing these very words now. I mumbled, *Not necessary.*

He simply stared at me. I reached for the backpack. *Please.* My hand touched the back of his. He let go of the backpack, and it fell onto its side. When I looked up again, he was off, walking forward with one leg describing a small circle at each stride.

Excuse me, excuse me, I murmured as I pivoted through the crowd. I held my backpack in front of myself, so I couldn't see the feet and legs I bumped and mashed. Zina's father glanced back at me. Zina had already put distance between us.

Near the exit, several men stepped almost in front of me. "Seer, taxi. Seer." I paused before bursting through the huddle around the door.

I thought of *No thank you* in Russian, barreled past a *babushka*, who continued to waddle without noticing. Outside the sidewalk simply disintegrated into the cracked pavement, no curb. "*Oi, blyad*," said my cursing father's son. The Zina inside me says that I should explain what a *blyad* is. It is somebody, usually a woman, who lost her way, she *zabludilas*. Sometimes the word is only *blya*, almost like *blah*, but with that *y* which slips into Russian vowels and lassoes the tongue. It means, "Oh, whore!"

My foot stomped somebody else's. My shoes would never pass as shoes from here.

I looked back. Zina's father stood hunched, while a woman harangued him, her finger pointed in the air, a young daughter crouched with hands patting the top of her foot.

When I came up to them and set my backpack against my knee, the woman began to chastise, and this language was too fluent for my ear. Its tone, however, was obvious. I caught the word *svoloch*, which I would learn means *bastard*. Her voice was raspy, deep, and male.

Why didn't you say excuse me? The little girl will step aside. You have big feet. You stepped on her foot, Zina's father said.

Excuse me, I said, making eye contact with the little girl, squatting and patting her foot. I'd lost the ability to shut my mouth. I said *Excuse me* again, and both Zina's father and the mother gave me the same nauseated look.

"*Excuse me, excuse me.*" Just go, "*debil*," said the mother. That last word means *moron*, which I first learned that day.

She yanked her daughter by the arm and hurried away, the girl limping faster even than her normal gait. The girl and I watched each other, never to meet again, two quivering gazes, tapering out like a child's mewl.

Zina's father looked over his shoulder at me. *In Russian, you have to speak loud.*

They say "Excuse me" here? I thought that Russians don't do that.

We're not Russians.

Ukrainians?

Odessans.

We approached a crooked huddle of men, one of whom leaned out. Zina's father hunched his shoulders and said to the ground, *Drive us to Economic and Nineteenth for fifty, and I won't tell anybody about it.* The man half-nodded and kept his head there as if reading the words Zina's father had said off the ground. He rubbed his chin. Still rubbing his chin, still looking at the ground, he began to walk away from the men. Every action was half done, a grifter's sleight of hand. Still rubbing and looking down, he crossed the street without checking for oncoming traffic. Zina's father followed and, without looking, waved at us to follow as well. Zina threw herself forward.

At a car, the man finally dropped his hand to open the door of a Mercedes. He put one leg in, halted, and wanded over the roof of the car. I followed Zina into the backseat. *Thank you*, I said as I climbed in, hugging my backpack.

Thank you for what? asked Zina's father.

I don't know, I mumbled. It seemed as if nobody was listening anymore.

On the way, I had practiced the phrase, *If necessary, I can find another place to spend the night.* Already on the airplane, I'd started to wonder about this whole journey.

When asked where to, Zina answered.

Oh, I see an Odessitka, the driver said back.

"Da," *is that what you see?* Zina snarled.

"Da," said the driver. His voice dropped. *I hear an Odessitka too.*

Zina wrapped herself tighter in her father's peacoat, shut her eyes, and lay back. The driver glared in the mirror. He was saying something about cabbage, probably how much they cost. Zina's father watched the road, shrugged here and there. The sunset that yawned across the flat landscape transformed Ukraine into the U. S. Midwest. The steppe leveled the sunset with the earth. The unnatural, or at least too simple, flatness appeared as if it were at the bottom of nature's diverse and varied beauty. As more structures appeared, more people did, more than in Detroit. There was no curb demarcating where the street ended and the road began. Small unpaved patches were simply trampled beds of traces of snow.

As we drove further, even more people began to appear in the streets. Our car squealed. The driver said something that made Zina's yawn begin to curl.

Later, when I asked what it was, she told me our driver had said to the driver who cut us off, *I hope a chimp shits in your mouth.*

Our driver pulled over. Zina's father was already out and approaching a kiosk along the road. A man wandered out from behind a building with his hand near his crotch, either adjusting his fly or fondling the fanny pack he wore.

He's buying cabbage. From where did you arrive? asked the driver.

I hesitated to answer. *I'm from America.*

"Hello, American! Why you not in hotel in center?"

It was the truth. *I don't have much money.*

No? And your uncle can buy cabbage for a lower price?

I said *he's not my uncle.* The driver spoke over me. Even though I understood each word, could even parse what I had heard back and forth, I didn't comprehend what was said until later. It was another one of those moments when I seemed to be missing some concept while I tried to translate in my head.

Zina's father sat down in the front with two cabbages in his lap. He set one on the dash and said, *Let's go.*

The car started moving again down the same road we'd been traveling before, tires squealing on turns. The driver said, *Welcome to Odessa.* Noticing how I shifted at each squeal of the tires, he said, *Better to die quietly, in sleep, like my grandfather, than screaming from horror like the passengers on the bus he drove.*

Zina's open mouth was up in the air. Something could fall in, while she was inhaling, and choke her. Must be nice, I thought. I couldn't sleep, no matter how beaten I was by exhaustion. Zina's father looked back and forth at the driver and the road on which we drove.

We turned and drove down a tiny alley toward a wall I thought we would hit before the car stopped abruptly and threw Zina's head toward the passenger seat. She clasped her face. The driver turned to Zina's father and held out his open palm. When he spoke, his words were only slurred breath and spittle to me.

Get out, Zina. We arrived, Zina's father said.

"No, Americans. Sixty," the driver said.

Zina's father only stared at him. Zina stirred, as if surprised by the English. Zina's father said something too low to be heard. I leaned forward to hear as Zina's father opened his door. The driver took Zina's father's elbow. *Zina, Valya, get out,* Zina's father said again. The driver yanked at his elbow. There was a dent in the blank wall of the building. A large crack interrupted the flatness. *Problem?* I asked.

"*Nyet,*" said Zina's father. With one hand, he gripped the cabbage so tightly that it creaked. He took the driver's wrist, and the muscles in his forearm flexed. *So rude to change the price after you picked us up.*

I fished in my pocket. Zina stopped me. *What's happening? Papa, let him go.*

I said fifty. He's trying to screw us.

You didn't understand Russian! the driver shouted

I held money out. "It's okay," I murmured. The driver released Zina's father's elbow and snatched the money. *Fifteen,* I said, accidentally, instead of *fifty.*

Ogling the money for a moment, the driver gritted his teeth. In what was more Ukrainian than Russian, he said, *Wha' you 'aid?* "Speak fah-cking English."

Fifty. Fifty rubles. "I mean, *griven.*" Zina didn't tell me at the time that I had mispronounced *hryven.*

No. I said seventy-five. You didn't understand. You can pay in dollars, not fucking rubles. Thirty dollars, said the driver.

Zina's father turned to sit facing the driver. *Valya, put your money away.*

I still had some dollars in a side pocket of my backpack. I found a twenty and handed it to him. It wasn't fifty dollars. Zina watched as if through a screen on the other side of the ocean.

This is enough, even with something for ice cream. You have a good boy, the driver said to Zina's father. The driver slipped the bill between his thighs and made a wave with the back of his hand and a little fart sound with his mouth.

Outside the car, I hefted my backpack again. As soon as Zina, the last of us to exit, was out, the car reversed and gunned out of the alley, squealing at another turn.

Zina's father glared at me. *I bought him a cabbage*, he said. *You gave him thirty-three times that sum.* Zina shrugged her shoulders and touched her father's arm on the same spot the driver had. *You Americans come here and throw your money around. He's a little mafia man. A thief, you understand? He always wants more.*

I had fixed it the American way, with a disproportionate amount of money about which I, as an American, was now supposed to complain, as if I had been robbed. My backpack slipped down from my arm again while we waited. "Sorry," I said, looking at Zina. She was obviously still half asleep. Zina's father looked at her. *Tell him not to give those people money.*

"Papa says you shouldn't give money."

"I know. I speak Russian too."

"I'm tired," she said.

Zina's father held on to his cabbage the whole time. He lead us around the corner of the building. Everybody was reading the sidewalk. I did too. There was a small stair with a ramp at its side. I shifted the weight of my backpack from one arm to the other, then I held it in a bear hug. Zina could still lead me wherever she wanted.

His thumb dug into several layers of the cabbage now, Zina's father jimmied the key. The smell of the car had settled into my clothes and hair. Watching him fiddle with the door, aware of Zina's zombie state behind me, I decided to say, *Thank you.* Zina's father grimaced. He could pretend he hadn't heard me.

Upstairs, a concrete echo was the only sound. The driver's "fahck" clacked in my brain. On the third floor we turned left three times in the hallway. Each door resembled the entrance to a bunker, designed against breaking and entering. Zina's father stopped at one, unlocked it, and the hinges grated. "Willkommen," he said.

Inside, a long hallway ended with a bathroom. The wooden floor had been scored, polished over. One room was large enough for three or four beds. It had only one now, a mattress on the floor. A large hutch cabinet in the corner displayed china. Otherwise, there were several ghosts in dusty white sheets. There must be an Abramovich anecdote about poltergeists, about them doing housework. The window was open, and outside cries of children skipped up from the courtyard.

This place was not home. I hadn't known a home for months. I had to stay awake as if my life depended on it. Zina rushed out of the room and flopped down somewhere else in the apartment.

I leaned my backpack against the wall. At the foot of the mattress on the floor, my knees buckled. I collapsed onto the loose mattress. Zina's father mumbled. I didn't understand. I heard the door slam and knew I was on borrowed time. Only my guilt kept me awake, and soon not even that was enough to keep me from submitting to exhaustion, a Russian word for which, *ustalost*, I didn't know then.

SIX

ZINA

In the room of her papa's apartment where Valinka slept, she
had seen on the table a book for tourists from the local library,
abandoned long ago. Like hipster urban explorers in Detroit,
her papa entered abandoned buildings and scavenged. Her papa
should go to Detroit. He would never leave Odessa. If he swindled
somebody, it was not for personal gain. He swindled for Odessa.
In this case, he collected some of the books from the abandoned
library before looters discovered it.

She remembered the librarian, Yevgeniya Yurevna. An older
woman, she had always been an object of attraction for Zina. Children sat on Yevgeniya Yurevna's lap in the kids' corner, and she let
them put their hands everywhere. Of course, this positioning became inappropriate as the children became older. Yevgeniya Yurevna had made Zina tingle like a tuning fork upside down.

Once she had heard faint voices in the library. At the end of one
aisle was a pipe, hissing through the floor. The pipe was installed
outside the wall, and holes cut through the floor were larger than
necessary. There was a gap where sound escaped. Whispers hissed
inside Russian consonants. Zina's step made the floor creak. The
voices ceased. Yevgeniya Yurevna swooped on her, even appeared
to fly over the floor. She didn't walk. *What are you doing? The library
is not a place to sleep standing!* Zina took her things and ran. She never returned. She never jerked off to Yevgeniya Yurevna again. She
simply lay there thinking about what happened. Yevgniya Yurevna was probably listening too. Zina spoiled it for her. The old bird
chastised Zina because Zina spoiled her espionage.

Ears whisper. These words Galya had said out loud. When Galya once caught Zina attending to what her parents were doing beneath the covers, Galya slapped her with a loose hand and did so with a smile.

This woman was from whom Zina had come. From whom had Valinka come? Galya would say of him, *He gives the finger with his hand in his pocket.* What had he said to her when he first met her? "You're for real." Because Zina was a language learner, these words were forever etched in her memory of the time and place when and where they were said, in the car on their way to Trumbulldome right after she arrived in America. What did they mean? Seeing Valinka asleep, like a boy the same age of his tender, stumbling Russian, she began to doubt her memory, doubt her understanding of Galya.

She returned to the present, the room where she had dropped all her baggage. Cold, she donned her papa's peacoat with АЛЕКСАНДР БОНДАРЕНКО in chalky Cyrillic along the inside of the bottom hem. When she closed it, the parallel rows of buttons on the breast appeared. She remembered Valentine gawking when he first saw this coat in Detroit. She had sized up what he was wearing. "What you dress?" she had asked.

"It's a holiday sweater. I only wear it once a year to take an annual photograph of myself in it. The sweater stays the same while the body inside it withers. I'm compiling a time-lapse series of photographs, in which I wear the sweater against a blank background over the years. I want to show the anachronism of identity politics." The words made her glad that he would no longer speak English now that he was in Odessa.

In Detroit, talk of identity politics was happening all the time. When Valentine's roommate Ben appeared, as payment, Zina offered him a five-pointed red star on a wheel. On top of the star was a disk at the center of which the Odessa Opera House was embossed. Around the border of the disk were the words ГОРОД ГЕРОЙ ОДЕССА. It was a trinket from some Odessa market, given to her by her papa as some shiny thing that could, perhaps, help lure a fish in America. Hearing the way these American leftists spoke, she wondered if it might work. She reached into her duffel bag to find it, took it out, and put it on the desk where Ben's items were. Ben sniffled. Zina asked, *Do you know what this is?*

As if offended, Ben said, *"Nyet."* He spoke Russian too. He had introduced Valentine to the language at Oakland Community College north of the city. He, it appeared, felt that he was the *"dyadya,"* the *uncle* patronizing Valentine's Russian, among other things.

It's an old badge from the war. Odessa became a hero city, Zina told him.

So? he said, turning his ear to her. He flipped it over and looked at the back. *Forty-four kopeck*, she thought to herself. Will he be able to date it based on the price? Surely he's not that canny about the Ukrainian economy?

I'll give it to you, she said. *Thank you for the floor.* She said this the way Americans thank veterans for their service.

Some Americans, like Lionel, would ask questions like, "Do they speak Ukrainian or Russian there?" and "Aren't they struggling to come out from under the Russian yoke?" This curiosity was good. It was healthy and helpful, and Zina wanted to answer Lionel's questions.

But other Americans, like Ben, had wanted to answer before her. His answers to Lionel's questions were, "Russian. I mean, some in the West of the country speak this weird language, a mix between Polish and Russian. That land has been speaking Russian for a long time. They really shouldn't even be a country," and "Don't confuse a bunch of fascist paramilitary rednecks with an indigenous people's movement, a struggle for independence. Ukrainian culture is made up, a conglomeration of Russian and Polish cultures, not a genuine indigenous movement. Although they have a right to be a free and independent nation, it doesn't mean it's a good idea. Before the real revolution, there's gotta be a bourgeois one." That was in December when Maidan was building up. Lionel would say simply Ukraine. Ben would say "the Ukraine," like "the sticks," where the rednecks live.

Valentine, whom she had begun to call Valya at this point, was neither kind of American. While Ben spoke about "the Ukraine," Valya opened his hands, peeked inside, and closed them again, as if he was disappointed to find nothing there. Ben had wanted her to feel betrayed. Instead she took pity on Valya, this failure of an Odessan. Lionel, Ben, they seemed to belong here. Valya didn't. He laughed, and the aspiration made a booger shoot from his nose onto the floor. Ben's pedantry made him blind to the booger. It stayed where it was, where Valya and Zina were supposed to sleep. She glanced out the rosette window. The void beckoned to her. Valya's ache to impress his friends, his roommates, for the time being at least, was like the exhaust remnants floating outside the rosette window above the streets. In the morning, it seeped in with the light, mottled by the stained glass of the window. The rays sharpened the bright advertisements of color on the cereal box Valya had told her was his, which he had never placed in the collective kitchen. Something about that light laced with that ache represented failure, as if its picture was next to *proval* in Valya's Russian dictionary, which lay on the desk next to his diary. In that diary Zina remembered reading the words, "My mind feels like a house. Every window is open to let the air flow throughout. The lights inside are all off. The light comes from the sounds outside, from where the breath of air comes. It knocks and flaps the small, hinged or hanging objects in the house. It closes doors, then throws them open again. The outside world enlivens the house."

When Ben said "the Ukraine" again, she asked him, "What would you do if price of eggs change from ten *hryven* to almost forty?" American Ben searched his lap as if he had dropped something right onto his penis.

In her room, her papa's office, she found the old typewriter that Galya had given to her. Language seeped down and out of her fingertips, through the glass of the keys, through the steel arm, across a layer of oil, which she applied from the tincture bottle Galya gave her, back into steel, into ink, dark like oxidized blood, pressed against the paper, newsprint, to which she would prefer something more pulpy, fleshy. She remembered the feeling of satisfaction when she made something slowly seep into the mechanism. She thought of all people, of any language, as merely slicing, tweeting language machines, after all. Clerical workers. Secretaries. Women. Even her papa was a woman when he used the typewriter.

Typewriters changed language, she decided.

In Detroit, they had also updated their language to make a new meaning. Ben's band planned a concert to mark the ninety-sixth anniversary of the October Revolution. They called the concert an "action." Those who would be on the platform, lower than a stage, were "actors," not performers, with the latter word's hint of exploitation. Those beneath were "witnesses" instead of audience members. There would be no catharsis for the witnesses, only a call to action. Something had to move. It wasn't a crowd, it was a gathering instead. When any of these terms was spoken, the speaker paused, emphasized it, and gave another pause afterward.

Zina remembered that night for another reason. That was when she had met Linda Cruz, the guitarist of Bulgakov Brothel, Ben's band. As the music clattered forward, its looseness matching the unbolted ruins of the Detroit landscape, the bassist and drummer took their places. When Linda Cruz stepped out, Zina said, "Lesbian."

What? Valya gasped in Russian. *How do you know?*

"I saw the way she put on guitar. Lesbian. I simply know."

When Ben came out pogoing and using words like *zemlyachestvo* and *narod*, words about folk culture, Zina rolled her eyes. Valya said, *When you roll your eyes, it looks like collapsing buildings.* He was trying to invoke her childhood, use it to be more than simply an

American. He wanted to have a hyphen before that descriptor. She would show him that such a childhood, her childhood, was not his. She would show him he did not know. And she would show off for Linda Cruz.

In Trumbulldome that night, somebody flipped a switch somewhere, and there was no light except that of the moon through the back window. When Zina went up again, it was as if the moonlight carried her. Her aura carved space among the witnesses. She twirled in a spin kick, something they had probably only seen Iggy Pop do. Childlike at the same time that it possessed the potential for danger, the kick could connect with somebody's jaw, render them mute. Maybe that was what people here needed — to shut up.

Her body, her twisting torso, was turning in the light, and this torrent made her appear almighty, a Greek punk goddess. Her presence was affecting the band. There was a smear from Linda Cruz' guitar string, like the scrape of jogging a vinyl album. After that the whole action sounded more murky, as if recorded once, then rerecorded at a slower speed, so that the sound washed in and out of coherence. Zina's eyes blazoned frenzy. She was seething. Ben thought he had power over Zina and Valya. But, like a fish caught, she could still move, flex her sharpened fin and frighten him enough, that he would lose that control over her. Ben spoke Russian that sounded like that of a Soviet official. *Na Ukraine* instead of *v Ukraine*, which was the way he said "the Ukraine" instead of simply "Ukraine," reminded her of a bad teacher who had told her, a fourteen year-old, that she would end up providing "services" on the Lanzheron Stairs. If Bulgakov Brothel was a nerdy literary reference and a stupid reference to a place such nerds would never show up, Zina would embody it. When Ben stuttered, it was clear that Zina could speak Russian that he had never heard, Russian from Ukraine, unofficial, raw, and unleashed Russian. And they would all simply smile from the side of their mouth.

That night she tore her shirt off, exposing her bra and bare
stomach, where — with black kohl she had taken from one of her
coworkers at McDonald's — she scrawled the word FeMen. This
reference she was sure nobody would know. In the middle of
a song, she grabbed Valya by the collar and asked, "Vhere you vas
on night of twenty-force September nineteen-forty-von?" The accent was exaggerated. Zina certainly knew how to conjugate the
English be for the second-person pronoun. However, it sounded
so much more authentically Russian if she didn't. The crowd was
surging, jeering, hopping around like Zina had, stopping when
she did. Ben frowned every time he caught glimpse of her. The
song began as low thrumming. It spun up into the chorus. Another hush muffled the crowd, like the snuffing of a once wildly gut-
tering candle. The puff of smoke retreating from the extinguished
flame passed over Zina's face, smeared with sweat. She thrust her
head at the ceiling, exposing her neck as if for the guillotine. She
climbed onto the stage and snatched the mic from Ben. They had
already passed the point of no return. Valya chuckled. He was
standing right next to her, only he was smaller. Watching him,
she said, "I don't recognize your institutions or your culture. It
don't matter to me." One witness had a handle of Mohawk vodka.
Zina snatched it from the witness' hand and drank from it. Ben
stood there, fuming. It was the way Americans fumed, as if they
can't believe what's happening to them. It didn't threaten Zina.
Nonetheless, they were at a crossroad. Somebody unplugged the
PA and switched on music. Ben crossed his arms, his elbows like
two buttons for Zina to push. He was about to gather his toys and
go home. She shrugged and handed him back the mic. The witnesses dispersed, shapes contrasting and pumping in the darkness. The only light shined bone-cold through a skylight cut in an
irregular shape out of the ceiling. From this skylight, splinters
hung overhead like whispers of the Sword of Damocles. Music
droned through the house. Zina was coming down from Olym-
pia. Her mystery was attracting Valya instead of Linda Cruz. He

moved nearer and nearer as if she were a black hole. He looked at her, she could tell, as if he wished he could see through her clothing. If she had seen him look this way when they first met at the empty lot near the airport bus stop, she would never have come to Trumbulldome with him. Now she could see through his clothing, all the layers of it, to his scrawny knobby nakedness. This thought made her shiver. At least she knew now with whom she was dealing. "It is cold here," she said.

That night, after she had indicated that she was cold, Valya had gestured at the door outside, to the backyard. Even though exiting the house was the opposite of what they should have done, something about the reversal, the inverse of sensibility, appealed to Zina. "Of course!" she screamed. Something was happening, urging her outside with Valya. She put on her peacoat.

Outside, the fire pit behind the house was cold. The chickens were already hiding in their coop. It was the ninety-sixth anniversary of the October Revolution, and Zina and Valya were standing by an outhouse. From that position, they could almost see the stars. Enough light had been extinguished in Detroit that it was sometimes possible to see cosmic luminescence, especially if you could get far enough away from the casinos. Valya was murmuring to himself. He looked at Zina, back at the stars, at Zina again.

He closed in for a kiss that night. "Eh," she stopped him the way a Canadian, not an Odessitka, would. "No," came from the lips he had almost kissed.

That night, in that moment, Valya's response was to flop to the concrete patio and flatten out against the cold stone. "Fuck," he said.

Listen, Valya, she began in Russian, since she was uncertain she could explain in English, *you need to know about me that I.*

You don't love me. "I mean, you don't like me. It's okay. I'm just an American after all. I shouldn't have tricked you."

Zina wished she had a cigarette. The smoke, the cold, it would all make the background of a fairy tale. "This like *skazka*. If we had a cigarette." Something needed to happen. She felt the need to give Valya something, even though she wouldn't touch any part of his body beyond his hand and whatever feeling he could register through all the layers of clothing. "Love," she said. During the action, her body had rolled and flexed and wound a shriek up inside her.

Now she let it out. Her tongue thrusted and ached in all directions, none in particular, flagged, became an open petal. Her face throbbed, skin went purple. When her shriek was swallowed in the cold night, she still gaped, taking in air for the next keening, which never happened. Her upper body appeared seized by electrocution. That was her answer to Valya's attempt at a kiss.

That night was the end of her time at Trumbulldome. When they stepped back inside, Ben told them that they could no longer live on the floor of his room. *Pity*, Zina said. He had been kind enough to pack their bags for them, the bags that now lay next to their beds here in Odessa. Zina's had been a life of migration and learning the language, the sound, of many, many different places.

On their way out, Linda Cruz, who had been sitting alongside the bassist on an old couch, made a click sound from the side of her mouth. "I heard you need a place to stay," she said.

Valya tried to speak. Zina interrupted him, "How much cost?"

"My family has an apartment. Couple hundred. It's just one room."

"You live there?"

Linda nodded. Zina shrugged, let her mouth fill with nothing. She set her bag down, dug into her underwear, and retrieved some paper money. She counted out two hundred dollars. Valya watched this retrieval and count as if his life depended on it. *With a lesbian?* he asked.

Zina frowned at him. *Why not?* She flashed her eyes at the guitarist and said, "Why not?" Already she was on her way to achieving the American dream that was of no importance to her whatsoever.

Linda grabbed the money and brought it to her face as if to sniff it. "Right on. That's what I'm talking about." Her eyes went up from Zina's feet to her hair and back down again. "I'm Linda. Linda Cruz."

"We met before," said Valya. Nobody listened to him.

With a smile, Zina took Linda's hand as if she had never seen that of a woman before. With her other hand, Linda grabbed Zina's and pulled her closer. "We're about to go to Ram's Horn to catch the sunrise. Want to come?"

To herself, Zina said, *Such a "Meksikanka."* Out loud, she said, *Good.*

"That means good," Valya said. Again, nobody listened to him. Why had she not listened to him?

Maybe if she had listened to Valinka, she would still be in America. Linda Cruz had been her ruin. No. Galya had been her ruin. No, her American voice said, you were your own ruin, bitch, pronounced *"beach."*

SEVEN

Valentine

woke in Zina's father's converted *kommunalka* apartment without any idea which of the twenty-four hours of the day it was.
On the table, conspicuous, as if put there for me as a kind of
itty-bitty joke, was a book called *Pure and Impure Odessa*. It was
something only Russian-speaking tourists would want to read,
a collection of detachable postcards of the city often called the

pearl of the Black Sea. One postcard displayed a perfectly proportioned girl, the Soviet Realist version of a Disney cartoon. She was hurrying away and leaving in her wake a boy who looked the same, only with shorter hair and boyish clothes.

When Zina entered the room, I already had a waking erection. Her presence made it become more permanent. She was wearing a long Chauncey Billups jersey, something it looked like she'd picked up from Linda and never given back, something very unlike the outfit of an Odessitka. Like an Odessitka, she shrugged her shoulders. I balanced the book over myself, so she wouldn't notice what was underneath. She snatched the book out of my hands and read the caption under the image of the boy and girl, *Teacher told Dasha that she had six apples. Okay, says Dasha. Now, says teacher, how many do you have if you give half to Dodik? Five and half, answered Dasha.* Zina frowned at the joke. "See," she said. "This don't work in English. Because there no 'a' and 'the.' You have 'half' and 'a half,' which are different meanings teacher and Dasha use for half." That an Abramovich anecdote might not work in English meant English couldn't understand Russian in its entirety. It was loss in translation, plain and simple. Even though I had roots here, every word I spoke was only a half. I was still straddling the threshold. Only one ear heard that side, the other left behind.

I lay back. The fuzzy math hadn't undone my hardness. If I got out of the bed, she'd see. I couldn't live that down. I'd slept next to her, in the same room with her, many times. My body was as confused as my language.

She was rummaging through a box in the room where I had slept. She was ripping through her past. *Here it is,* she said. "This is the journal of my papa. Written in third-face." *It's not Russian,* she said. I looked this up: *third face* is the Russian way of saying *third person,* like in a narrative.

What's not Russian? I asked. I was so happy that she was speaking to me in her language. English, now that we were in Ukraine, sounded illegal to me. Little did I know that soon there would be laws proposing that Russian itself be illegal.

That way, third person. I have such a condition, she said. "Everything is 'Zina does this, Zina does that.' I still not in first-face, like normal. I don't know which hour it is. I mean, whole twenty-four hours. I don't know which one we're in."

"Same," I said.

Ignoring me, she said, "My papa even give me the," and she said a word that, when I looked it up, was translated as *potassium bromide*. It had sounded like *kaly*, I remember. "To sleep," she said.

What's that? I asked.

She had picked up and was examining a typewriter. So, instead of answering about the *potassium bromide*, she said, "Typewriter with Baltic accent." I laughed, even though I hadn't understood. I thought a laugh might help soften my erection. "This a typewriter. From Germany. The Erika." She lifted up the Erika. It had glass keys, which looked as if they would slice in a machinated, soundless motion. They displayed the twenty-six letters of the Roman alphabet. "My mama give me this," Zina said. She smiled as if at a mushroom cloud. "You heard this anecdote? Those without father, they are like Jesus Christ."

"Immaculate conception," I said.

She pointed and shook her finger, said, "That!" and turned back to the Erika. "Mama want me to write on this." She broke into Russian. *Mama, I don't speak the language.* "Then they get me the lessons of English. But this man who teach me, he has horrible breath, like cabbage. He chews little spices." She crouched and put the Erika in front of herself. *Mama, I don't speak the language,* she said again. Her voice became deep and thunderous, threatening. *Then write in Russian,* the deep voice said. *How, mama?* She stood and faced me. She could either give me a lecture or seduce me. "We made the system. These letters and numbers can be Cyrillic. Look," she gestured for me to approach. I could feel that my penis was flaccid, finally. She rolled a piece of paper into the

Erika. "For bread, you type like this." She typed x/le6. "You see? Or this. Here is 'and.'" She typed N. "This *I* is backwards. For lower case, you type U. Rose is like this." She typed роза. "Bread and rose." The deep voice possessed her, said, *You can use this skill to make money, dear.*

Her face changed as if she saw something that I didn't. *Is there a poltergeist?* I asked, proud to know the word for poltergeist.

I would have learned, mama. For America, Zina said. The deep voice said, *No, dear.* Zina's gaze followed the poltergeist as she passed through the floor. There Zina's gaze stopped. Zina snapped out of it and said, "My papa says typewriters are just for women."

Then why does he still have a typewriter? Typewriters brought the Revolution! I said. She made a quick roll of her eyes and left the room.

When I finally emerged from my bed, I was wearing earbuds. Zina's mouth moved. It looked like a curse, and I whisked the earbuds out, afraid I had missed something. "Good morning," I said. She shrugged to dismiss my greeting. I was beginning to become used to this gesture. I was learning to overlook it. I had read an explanation of the Odessan shrug in *Pure and Impure Odessa:* an American tourist who knows a little Russian asks, *Where is the State Opera House?* Abramovich — whom the American asked — holds up his parcels to the tourist, who takes them. The American thinks he'll use his hands to show the way to the Opera House. But, once his hands are empty, Abramovich merely shrugs his shoulders and shows his upturned palms.

I made breakfast, Zina's father said, *but we already ate. Come this way.* When I hesitated, he said, *What? You follow my daughter to Ukraine, but you won't follow me into the kitchen?* He slapped his hand against the frame of the door into the kitchen. *The kitchen is sixteen meters square,* he said. *Plenty of room for you. I should have some of those headphones too, ones which translate, in order to understand when you speak English. But you speak well enough in Russian. Unless you want to speak English?*

No, papa. He listens to music through the headphones. She narrowed her eyes at me.

"*Muzika?*" said Zina's father.

I held the earbuds up to him, which he examined before poking into his ears, harder than was necessary. He winced, furrowing his brow, amusing Zina. Her laugh carried into his. He took them out, and one of the pads of the earbud remained in his ear. He said, *Very primitive, Valya. We have it better here.*

Zina laughed again, said, "We have it better here."

Her father served me eggs. *Just like in America, no?* I sat down, and they watched, waiting for me to eat. I moved to do so. The eggs were watching too. He was digging in his ear. *Do you love to eat eggs in America?*

Zina turned to me. "He really doesn't know any English."

He sat back and crossed his arms, hmed at us. *I can try.*

Watching him, Zina leaned toward me and said, "My papa don't want to learn lingua franca of modern times — English. I think he needs therapy." I thought, Which kind of therapy, Zina? I answered my thought in English. He would do narrative therapy. Like I was doing. I was redoing the narrative of my life. So far, my life hadn't kept anybody reading or listening.

If he speaks Russian, why should I learn English? her father asked. I shrugged the Odessan way. Nobody noticed. I lifted my fork and poked the eggs. *Valya, why did you come to Ukraine? Do you have relatives here?*

One aspect of my personality, which I was trying to change, was that I spoke without thinking, even in a language foreign to me. Such is the state all foreign language speakers wish to attain. There's a risk. To answer his question, I said, *No relatives. I didn't have anything to do.* Their stares shrugged at me, wanting more. *I think,* I sighed, *I'm in love with your daughter.* For Zina's father, I used the formal, the *vous.* I didn't presume any familiarity. *She's my only connection with this place.*

They locked eyes with one another. Her father had an aura around him. It seemed difficult to tell why he was piqued, whether out of anger or out of some reckless joy. After I said I was in love with his daughter, this aura became reduced to a line. I braced for his attack. The line snapped, and his laughter rose in pitch like a doomsday siren.

At least it wasn't anger. Zina was laughing too, and the only tears I ever saw there formed in her eyes, into which I looked so deeply. *Oh, dear. What will we do with you, good boy?* her father asked.

I waited for the laughter to calm down a little before I said, *I have Russian roots.*

Zina, who saw I was serious, took a bite, pointed with her fork at herself and her father, who was still cracking up, and said, "But we not Russians."

Ukrainian roots, I corrected.

"Odessans." She watched me. She put a small bite of food in her mouth, tried not to laugh. She tried as hard as she could. It didn't work, and she had to put her fork down and even spit out her food to prevent from choking.

I wanted to get out of the USA, I said.

"*Da?*" he said, which started a whole new chorus of wicked laughter from both of them. Each one outdid the other, only to be outdone by the next wave. Each time this happened, I sank further into my seat. The laughter silenced me. I decided I should wait until it ended. That was the best way to learn, to shut up and hear. Not even to listen, to let the sound cross me like a wave.

I was able to finish my eggs. I was able to drop my fork on the plate. I was able even to see myself in the greasy reflection on the ceramic. As the laughter finally petered out, as it turned into snickers, and hooting calls, and Zina wiped her eyes for the last time, the room became silent. I wanted them to experience that too. So I waited. There were noises from her father's neighbors behind the walls. I wanted to ask *Is this a "kommunalka?"* I didn't want to be the first to speak. My Adam's apple bobbed.

First Zina's grin faded, her father's second. Once those grins were gone, once there was no longer any joy at my expense on their faces, I opened my mouth. I opened and asked what I'd wanted to about the communal apartment. This question prompted the second longest amount of time people have spent laughing at me, the first being the moment prior. Her father gaped at the space in front of himself, leaned forward so that his elbows touched his knees, clapped his hands together and held them in a throbbing shake. He screeched laughter. To Zina he shouted, *I understand why you brought him. Everything he says is golden!* It was a catastrophe. I crossed my arms as if to defend myself. I waited and listened. It hurt. I was learning through pain how to speak in this new world to which I'd come. The pain was helping me to cross the surface. Pain, says Marx in Das Kapital, is necessary for development. The humiliation was my measure of humanity.

Zina coughed and cleared her throat. She was trying to become serious. "It used to be, probably." A titter erupted. "But my papa converted it." A deep sigh fell in tone. "Yes, this the famous communist kitchen. People so close they become enemies. They live right next to their enemies all the time." She looked at me. It was as if to make sure I was listening to this part in particular. "It's the Soviet way. People never break up. They never part ways. No matter how much they make the fun of the other. No matter how much we laugh at you."

Zina twitched, turned to her father. *Now, probably, you wish you learned English, huh?*

Still laughing, he said, *I understand everything. Except one thing.* He turned to me and, wincing, asked, *Who chooses to come to Ukraine without family, without the language, without anything but my Zina?* He waited a moment before saying, *It's a bit strange. But it's okay. You brought my Zina back.*

I brought him, papa. Zina turned back to me. "Nobody wants to go to Midwest, right? It's as bad as Ukraine. You come from one *mukhosransk* — this means shithole — to another." Zina already knew what I'd say. She started again. "The fly-over states." There was a kind of performance going on. The other Zina, the Zina I thought I knew, said to me, Be careful. Don't bring me out of the closet in front of my father.

As if she was reading my thoughts, typical for Zina, she did what she needed in order to throw me from any understanding of her that I might pursue. She shifted eye contact from me to her father. *Papa, why is my name Zinaida?* she asked. The question sounded as if asked before, the answer forgotten.

Her father's reverie dropped off a cliff. He winced at his tea. For some reason, his fun was over. *Why Zinaida? Well, that comes from my days in the Navy. After serving on a cruiser called Admiral Makarov, I was transferred to a destroyer called Zinaida.* He sipped more tea. *Take your elbows down. Like an American…*He gaped at me as he sipped again. *We always thought that the boat was named after some kind of mysterious woman whom some sailor knew.*

And what, pop? Was that it?

He winced at her this time. He watched her for a moment before, as if addressing his tea, he answered, *Don't know. After the Fall, I returned here. But I always loved that name.*

"Oh, papa. That sucks," she said to him. She tapped the table. The breath she took could have been a sob. As she walked away, I realized her gait was different. It was softer. Her heels raised, her weight was supported only on the balls of her feet. It was an awkward, child's gait, quieter than before. "I hope you two will be able to communicate," she tossed over her shoulder as she walked away, boyish and girlish at the same time.

Her father jumped up to follow behind and stop her in the hall. He whispered and stuffed his hands in his pockets. I peeked through the kitchen door.

Zina shouted over his shoulder, "You must help keep tabs on my papa. He will run off to drink and visit the brothel. You know. Crazy Russian. Like in Dostoyevsky. He don't know how to hide browse history."

It was nice of her to say that. It made me smile, which I no longer wanted to do in front of her, at least not without thinking. I was successful, in that moment, at changing the narrative of my life. I wanted to talk about what was really on my mind. I wanted to be able to bring anything up, even if it hurt the person with whom I was talking. I thought that's what Zina did.

Zina's father looked over his shoulder at me and, while he did so, Zina leaned forward and kissed him on the cheek. *I'll sleep more, papa.* He deflated as she slipped through the door to her room.

I remember thinking about that attempt at reconciliation, when I returned to the kitchen, turned on the water, and screamed. The water was scalding hot. The dish soap label, written in cursive Cyrillic letters, displayed a burly sailor who glared at me. I heard the voice of the Zina I thought I knew say, It will always be so. You can never take our light steam. It's too intense for you.

EIGHT
ZINA

She would have to get used to him again, her papa's constant presence, marked by the stumbling sound he made when he cleared his throat. She would have to get used to his little puffed breaths again. Her papa sat in the kitchen, petting the tablecloth with his skinny hands. The sound of petting was like panting. All because her mama used to dribble her fingers there. If Zina reminded him of those dribbling fingers, he would go pale as if his blood had gone down a well plumbed drain.

Once, when she was a little girl, she had come up to him and said, *When will it be just you and I, papa?* That was how she had cursed them. Galya left soon after she said that. Galya left. *What happened and who's guilty?* was a commonly heard question in Odessa. *I*, she would say. *I'm guilty. But I'll never apologize.*

After moving into Linda Cruz' basement in Southwest Detroit, she had decided to try to write to her mama. The only point of contact Zina had for her was an email address. The idea that she would find Mama by whims about cars was like the way some village rube would come to Odessa to find his long-lost papa. It was a dream. The problem with the dream went like this: she extinguished the desire to see Mama; she knew that what always happens next is what is least expected; she extinguished the desire and tried hard not to expect it ever to happen; now that it was least expected, it would come true; she was expecting it again; it would not happen; it would never happen until she no longer remembered Mama whatsoever; by then, Mama would be dead. It was an impossible dream.

She would hear Mama's greeting, *Zdorovo*, and she would lift slightly off the ground. She needed to move forward in her life. Unrequited Mama love was not forward.

So she spent half a day in Detroit composing a missive, her life story after Mama left. She even used some words from Mama's native tongue, *surzhik*, Russian spoken with Ukrainian words, like the language spoken in Mama's native Poltava. For instance, Mama would say things like *bachit* instead of *smotret*, the word for look. She would say *yak* instead of *kak*, the word for how. Instead of *esli*, she wrote *khai*. The word for *want*, conjugated for the first person, *khochu*, Mama pronounced the Ukrainian way, emphasis on the *kho*. After rhetorical questions, those of which she already knew the answer, to emphasize, she wrote the word *ili*, which is the Russian word *or*. When said alone after something obvious, something the speaker should have taken for granted as understood already, it was an Odessanism. In this soft language, Mama would read Zina's laments. Maybe Mama would braid her hair while she read out loud and in her own Ukrainian voice. *Ili.*

Zina only left out one event and pressed SEND.

Mama immediately wrote back in English, "This is all great and wonderful to hear! But why not on English? I dont know if I speak this no more. Anyway, great to hear from you. Unfortunately, I cannot go all long way to Detroit. Take care, Mama."

Zina remembered thinking, *But how "long" a way was it really?* Zina would be happy even with a radius. She imagined her typing "Galina," or "Gala," or "Galya," or whatever her mama was called in this country. It didn't matter. Zina imagined Galya sitting in a nice apartment with a nice computer, which Galya wasn't allowed to use. Zina saw Galya delete "Galya" and type "Mama," click send, and jump up to tiptoe away when she heard a cough from the man with whom she lived. This man probably jokingly called Galya "comrade." He probably made a stupid face and asked Galya to marry him. He probably asked her to promise to be true, whatever that means to an American. He probably promised to take her home to Odessa, that they could have one wedding with his fat family and another in a church with a harmonious, Orthodox dome. She probably said, "No. It is not necessary."

Zina's English had needed to be better or at least as good as Galya's. She had needed to defeat the American Dream in its own language.

Here she was in Odessa again, sitting at the empty typewriter Galya gave her, typing words that would never reach Galya, would never reach anybody, words that only fed back into her mind. She typed *don't cry don't cry don't cry never cry you lived long enough don't want don't want don't want never want remove want you wanted enough.*

From the kitchen her papa asked her, *Zinochka. Why do you type on that? Why not send an email?* To write on paper, put it in a box, and know that it carried her voice through the world was supposed to be cathartic. All the same, Galya was gone. Galya was gone like how the end of an aria quits in the throat of the singer and floats off the streets around the Opera House and worms upward. No matter how poetic her letters to Galya, Galya was gone.

To joke about this absence was as impossible as Russian on a German typewriter without Cyrillic. *I like the physical presence,* she yelled back at her papa. *And mama gave it to me.*

His silence was as long and loud as his voice was. "*Da,*" was all he said to end it. *I should sell it.*

God no, she shouted, *besides, who'll buy it? Nobody here can allow themselves to be a "connoisseur" of typewriters. You need money? I have some money, papa.*

He entered the room and asked in a quieter voice, *What's a "kan-iu-siur"? Like surrealism?*

She said to herself, *Did I really come from this man?*

Zinka, what if I send her money sometimes?

"*Chto?*" Again she was on shaky ground, again on the whirring, listing airplane. *Why?*

He said, *Maybe she wants to return?* and shrugged. At least he could still shrug? She knew he would die before he'd stop sending her money. *Ili.*

Wait. You know where she is? Which address? If she had known an exact address...

San Francisco.

You knew she was in San Francisco? So why did I go to Detroit? Her papa stared at the typewriter, the blank page within it. She heard Valinka walk the floor of his room and worried that her papa would soon close this conversation. *You didn't want me to find her.*

I wanted you to go to the worst part of the country. That's what I heard. That's where I wanted her to be, in the worst of America. I needed you to go there so you would come back. Get it?

In the other room, Valinka was reading M words out loud: "*...mukha, mukholovka, mukhomor, muchenie...*" *fly, fly trap, death cap mushroom, torment.*

She did not remember putting on her shoes and coat. She did not remember descending the stairs. She did not notice her surroundings until she was in the courtyard. She was still not noticing the journey, only thinking of what had set her off on the journey. If she had known where Galya lived when she was in America, she could have traveled there. She could have found Galya. Galya would not have been an abstraction, like revolutions, countries, democracies, essences. These female things didn't die easily. Bodiless, they tossed themselves further into the future. A female abstraction changed hands, sold herself to the highest bidder. Female nouns would remain long after everybody. Odessa was another. The future is female, she thought. The future is for pussies.

Now she could find Galya. Now she could kill her if she could return to America. Her papa did not have Galya's exact address. He had a location — a Western Union, where he was sending her money. She could kill him for what he had not done. In the courtyard outside the building, an old man, named either Borya or Kostya, sang, *The sea seems like the sky/ let's throw anchor.* All her papa had needed to do was tell her one small piece of information. Instead, his deep, pounding heart had sucked her back to Odessa. She wanted to crush her papa, shatter him with her sound that would carry across the wavelets of the Black Sea and threaten the shores of Russia. Or simply not let him tell her anything anymore. An orphan now, nobody could tell her what to do. Grandmas would shut their windows. Now that she had returned, she would rewrite the whole story. Her papa, like all the people in this country, was traumatized and, in turn, traumatized everybody he touched. To reverse the trauma, she would have to stop joking, stop saying things merely in pieces. The whole future would need to be wide open and clear. *Ili.*

Through the *proyezd* she left the courtyard. She was unsure she would ever return through the passageway into the courtyard of the building where her papa lived. On the other side of it was this new Odessa, which she had always defined by her papa and lack of her mama. Now it was defined by her papa alone since she knew where Galya was. That this knowledge of her papa's had lived here in this place, in the very quarters she had shared with him so many years, and not revealed itself to her felt like the utmost betrayal on the part of Odessa. In the end, she had thought that it had been some kind of Odessan anecdote, some joke, and her mama would come smiling out from some hiding place somewhere in the city Zina had scoured during her youth. But Odessa had lied to her. Or Odessa had let her believe a lie Zina herself had created. In the end, Odessa was her mother, like the anecdote about Abramovich goes. *Where do you come from?* was a question asked about parents. But the answer for her was, truly, *from Odessa.*

She knew she would have to change this country, that of her birth.

She had already proven herself in America. While in Detroit, early one morning close to New Years, she had climbed into the very back seat of a minivan with Valya. The other seats had been taken. Linda had demanded they take part in a protest outside a Michigan women's prison where a doctor was performing sterilization. "One woman said they basically melted her ovaries," said Linda. She had brought a guitar and wanted to perform a song with Zina there.

On the way, Valya looked back and forth at Zina and the road. "You're on a work visa," he had said.

Even though he had been right, Zina shrugged. She had taken with her a sack of food from her job. Inside were fries so sopping with oil they did not crunch and patties nobody called meat anymore. Why had she been in America working at McDonald's? She remembered when the first McDonald's opened in the Soviet Union in Moscow, how her papa traveled there by train twelve hours and returned twelve hours later having acquired such fries as those she ate that day. The burger would have been too much. After all those hours of travel, the fries had become cold potato fragments. Nonetheless, how they had savored them with knife and fork! No American could understand that smack of satisfaction.

That day in rural Michigan, like an American, Linda had balked and called across the van, "That's what you're eating?"

"Food is food," Zina had said over her shoulder.

"That's not food. It's grease and inflammatories," Linda had replied.

Zina had turned to Valya. "My inflammatories taste good. Yours?" She remembered putting a fry in his mouth and trying to read Linda's reaction.

Linda had made a face and said, "Blech."

To Zina, it had sounded like *blyad*. She had said, *You hear, Valya? She said "Whore."*

Later, when she said, "Linda, your driver brake too powerful," Valya asked her back, *You drove in Odessa?* She had recently received her license in America, so she answered, "Yes. Here and in Odessa. Since I was small child."

Linda had said, "Gringa chingada," to the window and, beyond it, to the Michigan plain.

Valya had mumbled to her, *You don't worry?*

"About what?"

About arrest.

"Why I should worry?" she asked him back in English.

Why do you speak to me in English? Valya asked.

"I need to practice." She laughed.

"Why are you laughing?" He waited for her to answer.

"Okay. I stress out you. Okay."

What's "okay"? Valya shouted.

"You," she grinned. "You're okay."

"You're fucking evil."

"A little bit," she kept grinning, "it's true."

His chin poked toward his lip like a microphone. He sighed. *I'll speak Russian, you English,* he said.

"Good," she said. *You understand?*

"*Nyet.*" Again, he waited. "How long will this go on?"

"If we are both from Odessa," she said.

I still don't understand. She remembered Valya making a face that had looked the way a stumble sounded. He tried to laugh, took breath in. His whole demeanor collapsed. Valya ran spindly fingers through his hair. He wriggled, blushed, and his sigh sounded as meaningful to her as a fart in a dress.

The sky had been gray and foggy. There had been a chance of rain. In front of the prison, at the end of a stand of trees, a crowd of people had gathered, holding signs in the air, the rhythm of a chant audible. The panting of human anger was audible. As they walked toward the chanting people, she had noticed that Valya's face was crumpled. Linda she couldn't hurt at all. Valya was a brittle branch.

She wished she had done everything the right way instead of the exact opposite of how she was supposed to be. She was supposed to love men. And men were not supposed to be like Valya. They were supposed to be strong and not talk too much.

Linda had gone to the front immediately and switched on the mini-amplifier clasped to her belt, weighing her pants down so that her butt crack appeared. She had said something in Spanish that made the people there stop chanting and become quiet. Observing this, Linda had turned to Zina. "Should we play that song we been working on?" She had begun to play the riff of a song by *Kino*. The song, *Change*, starts with a troubled, regular rhythm, like the sound of the chant. Zina began to sing the Russian song. A woman shivered. When Zina got to the chorus, Linda shouted in English, "We wait on change!" The sound was sharper than the guitar. Linda had fired Ben for inauthenticity. Now she was trying to co-opt this Soviet song. But, in English, the song didn't sound right. Viktor Tsoi sang this in the Soviet world of 1988. Americans were too impatient. Zina observed the guards who had come outside to watch them. Each of them had a smug smile. These bitches didn't deserve to have children. The smiles stretched up to the guards' ears and closed the ear canal, so sound didn't travel to their brains while they wore such masks. These smiling masks grinned harder as the crowd migrated into the road. When the protesters spilled into the street and traffic met them and had to stop, she looked back at the guards. One took out his phone and said a couple words, hung up.

After that call, the police showed up with the same kinds of grins. With zipties, they handcuffed Zina and seated her on a curb of the parking lot. She avoided Valya's eyes.

A black truck arrived to pick them up. It was like the "bread trucks" in the Soviet Union, generations ago. Everybody had known they held people inside. Everybody had called them *crows*. She thought her life in America would end inside a *crow*. She would ride to the police. They would seat her, book her, and send her away. They would not send Valya there. Valya had a document that said he was a full-fledged American.

Now her papa was so happy that she was back in prison with him.

Valinka found her in the courtyard. She began to recount to him about how she stole her mama's cigarettes from her purse. *She said to me, "You smoke those cigarettes, and I'll come and find you and give it to you on the cheek." She was angry the way an adult is angry at another adult, even though I was only seven years old. I didn't want to smoke them. I only wanted my mama not to smoke them. I put one in my mouth, kissed it, pinched it between my fingers, and said, "I'm smoking." Like a mime.*

It was unclear whether Valinka was listening. He might have been too afraid to listen. "When mama was angry with me, she made her voice low. You seen the cat with her ears back? My mama try to grab me. I escaped. I ran outside, down the steps, through the courtyard, to the sea. After such a run, you don't want to smoke cigarettes no more. But mama's voice chase me. It was not like the voice of a mama. It was like the voice of a woman to another woman, to an adult. You understand?"

You said that already, in Russian, said Valinka.

"But I mean, the voice chase me. The voice." *You understood? When I came home, her voice was normal again. Her voice told me to eat and lie down. In my bed, lights turned off, I heard her voice again. I understood by the sound of her voice that she was smiling. I could hear the smile. She didn't want to smile. But she was amused. Her voice groaned like a teenage boy. It sounded like the voice of a daredevil. Without fear.*

I understand.

You understand? When mama left us, that voice remained. I took it into my own sound. That voice helped me deal with the "zadira" at school, a girl who-.

What's a "zadira?"

"The bully. She called me shameless. Her voice sound older too. Papa can't do this voice. Even now he don't talk to me like an adult."

Don't speak English, Valinka said, gritting his teeth and staring into the soil.

"Sorry. Mama probably speaks English now. So the voice, it is now English. It talks the way Americans do. You, well, you not American enough. But you kind of got it. Americans talk cocky and stupid. Maybe mama even lost her accent. That is the voice for me too. I try to do this American voice." *This voice tunes me. The voice comes from within. You still understood?* Tears edged Zina's eyes. A sob nudged her to spill. She could hold it. She could hold it until she knew Valinka would hear it exactly as it needed to be heard.

Her time in America did not end in the *crow*, the truck labeled *BREAD*, the police van. Out the window, she saw a trailer with a horse inside. Zina could see through the window the horse's head and long, fine mane, which whipped in the wind. When she yawned once, her mama asked, *Do you like horses?* Zina answered, *Of course, mama. Why, Zinochka? Because, mama, horses are strong and work hard. True*, her mama answered. *Zinochka, the only difference between a horse and a human is that a human can last longer than a horse at work.* When Zina gaped at her, her mama said, *Keep going. Don't stop.* She never stopped all the way to the West.

It did not even end at the police station, where they filed out of the truck and into the lobby. There the cops had set out a folding table to book the protesters as fast as possible. Standing in line, Valya began to grunt, the way he did when he concentrated on what he was reading. He came close to her, even bumped into her from behind. He was too nervous, she could tell, to speak Russian. She would return home in flames, crackling like the sound of the Russian *S*. "ID?" the cop asked. She handed over her license. There it was, ZINAIDA BONDARENKO, in Roman letters. She had prayed that they would not take it away from her, that she would be able to bring one souvenir home to papa. He handed it back to her and said, "ID?" to Valya. She filed behind the others into a cell.

When Valya came and sat next to her, he was no longer grunting. He panted as if his heart had run from the prison to the station. What had happened? She had said nothing, and the good law enforcement officer had assumed that this gorgeous young white woman was an American citizen.

In the cold jail that night, the light had made her skin sizzle. It was cold, almost as cold as the bony snow outside. Nothing stuck out or interrupted the quiet. Every noise carried to every ear. Zina felt the hustle opening within her, an approaching rev. "Detroit hustles harder," people say. While in Detroit, she learned that, usually, the people who say these words are not actual Detroiters themselves. "Odessans hustle still harder," she said out loud. "Odessitkas hustle harder than them."

Valya shushed her and said, *How can it be that they don't know that you're a foreign woman? It won't be for long. They'll check on a computer.* He blinked several times and said, *You understand? We're fucked.*

"Why we? You not fucked, my friend."

Hearing the English, Valya shushed her again and looked in the direction of the officer guarding them. He closed his eyes and exhaled, and the exhale sounded like a desperate prayer. *Listen,* he said. *I don't want to be separate from you. I thought they'd take you away.*

When Galya left them, she and her papa went to the beach in Arkadia. They stood there, her papa staring at a rock big enough to sit on. He said that, when he was a boy, he would sit on a knitted shawl on that very rock on this very beach, a little south of Odessa. She could hear the Black Sea, hear the grunts of her papa, a boy, shivering and trying to hide it.

As they finished their cigarettes and stepped back inside the apartment building, she looked at Valinka and saw a skinny, shivering boy. His weakness, his vulnerability, these things once kept her warm in a dark, silent cell. Now they would keep her warm in Odessa. That had not been the end. They could have deported her after the arrest. She had wondered how these Americans became so rich and powerful when they acted like such idiots. Valinka said, *When I was in* "Occupy Detroit" *in* "Grand Circus Park," *I learned how fires and cigarettes clean up tear gas. Did you know that because you're from here?*

Even though she didn't, she nodded as if she did. Valinka was a boy too, and he too would weaken and, as they say in Russian, *clean off.* She wanted him to believe that all his desires lay here, across an ocean and steppe, on the shore of the Black Sea, far from his home. Why not? She had believed something similar about America. *Nobody misses you in America? Not mama? Not papa?*

Mama probably misses me.
"She don't want you back?"
When I first moved out, she packed me condoms. And papa...
Understood.

In Odessa, there was a Western Union. Earlier, a Dagestani sold kebab there. *How did Odessa change?* Galya might ask. In 2014, there were so many skinheads from the East striding around, that they would say of Odessa, *All they do there is shave their heads and die.* War had still not called Odessans to action with the exclamation, "*Ura!*" It was the time of year when students would lean back yet straighten their torso, raise one hand in a pitched Nazi salute. Of course, that was not what was meant. It was a horizontal, drunken hug.

Zina wanted to send Galya a farewell. She had crossed the ocean for Galya. She had learned English for Galya. The rest of her life would pass without Galya. These dull sentences she had known now for a long time. Only to know them was not to let them be her whole story. There had been a long period of repeating English to herself, sounding it out and listening to her voice speak it, before she could understand. There had been mistakes. Once she had accidentally referred to a cigarette butt as a butt, period, asking other English speakers, "Where do I put my butt?" There had been gaping responses to her new words, the new way she rewrote her story. She had raised her voice, cursed herself, corrected, and spoken clearly in English. She had commanded the story of herself. Words such as, *Mama doesn't love me*, created a simple sentence that nonetheless carried meaning deep into a person, blasted them from inside out.

The kiosk was empty when she stepped up. A small man emerged. He was chewing, and there was a thin mustache above his lips that moved like the surface of an angry sea. *I'm listening.*
Greetings. I want to send a telegram.
Telegram? From which century are you?

I want to send a telegram, she repeated. Galya always said to her, *Repetition is the mother of education.* She repeated herself to the man a third time.

All right. All right. The man stepped behind the wall and emerged again with a machine, presumably what he would use to send a telegram. *I need to hook it up. Also, you're savvy that this only works in English? Only the punctuation is in Cyrillic.*

She had not been aware of that. Galya answered emails in English. *All right.* She tried to sound like he did, tried to catch the apathy that his speech schlepped into utterance.

It's gonna cost a lot, he said.

How much?

If your voice was money, you'd lose your voice.

All right.

```
27 FEBRUARY 2014
GALINA FEODOROVNA PODOLSKAYA


DEAR MAMA ЗПТ


HAPPY BIRTHDAY ВСКЛ
DONT CRY ЗПТ MAMA ТЧК I DONT THINK YOU WILL SEE
ME AGAIN ТЧК I TRIED TO COME TO YOU ТЧК BUT I FAILED
ТЧК YOU FAILED TO FIND ME ТЧК

YOU FAILED TO OPEN YOURSELF ЗПТ MAMA ТЧК YOU HID
YOUR SELF FROM ME ТЧК BUT I DONT HIDE ТЧК I FEEL ТЧК
PAPA STILL DONT BELIEVE YOU GONE ТЧК I BELIEVE ТЧК
I SEARCHED ANOTHER MAMA ТЧК I SEARCHED ODESSA ТЧК
I SEARCHED U ТЧК S ТЧК A ТЧК THERE IS ONLY ONE MAMA
ТЧК

BECAUSE OF THIS ЗПТ I WILL NEVER BE MAMA ТЧК

WE WOULD BE PODRUSHKI ЗПТ IF YOU STAYED ЗПТ MAMA
ТЧК INSTEAD OF EMPTINESS ЗПТ I WOULD COME UP TO YOU
AND MY ARMS WOULD GO AROUND YOU AND WE WOULD EMBRACE
```

TЧК I WOULD KISS YOU MANY TIMES ON EAR TЧК I WOULD
DEAFEN YOU WITH MY KISSES TЧК YOU DID THAT ONCE TЧК
    THANK YOU ЗПТ COMRADE ЗПТ FOR A WONDERFUL CHILD-
HOOD ВСКП

    YOURS FOR LONG ЗПТ NOT ANYMORE ЗПТ
    LOVE ЗПТ
    ZINOCHKA

Her power ached like that of a bruised victor as she returned
from sending the telegram. She could hear Galya giggling when
she would first glance at it. Zina passed a corridor between blocks
where a wind from the Black Sea passed through and deafened
her. Galya, in Zina's imagination, stopped giggling and slowly began to frown. Slowly, with the telegram, Zina gained power over
Galya, power Galya had taken from Zina by leaving her behind.
Zina announced her strength, and it worked. She had gone to Detroit. Galya would have run from Detroit as if the city was on fire.
It had been foolish to go there in search of Galya. Now Zina had
nothing to lose.

One morning in Detroit she had set out to explore, even started running. At a street corner, right before she turned and set
off on another sprint, she heard somebody yell out, "Is that for
real? Those tree hugger kids." It was so early that the sun was only
a small distance above the horizon. Her American voice had been
giving her directions like, It's all fucking backwards. You should
of turned left back there, not right. No biggie, though. You ain't
going nowhere.

Two men walking toward her split to let her pass between.
When she tried to go to the side of one of them, he moved in front
of her. She smashed up against his chest, which smelled like the
floor of Trumbulldome. He laughed as she shook off her surprise.
The other man said, "Give me all your money." Zina turned to him
slowly, in a way that suggested that within her were well-oiled

mechanisms which made heavy, silent movements. "You heard me, bitch." He said it like a bitch. His voice dropped the last word as if he had realized as he said it that the difference between himself and her, his penis, was hanging flaccid right now, merely a doughy piece of flesh, nothing much to fear.

I don't understand you, she said in Russian.

The man, into whom she had literally run, elbowed the one speaking. "*Den-gi*," he said and rubbed his fingers together in front of his chin, the international sign for money.

Zina shrugged and made a gesture of opening her hands, palm up, in front of herself. This gesture was the international sign for *don't got*. It was a variation of the Odessan shrug.

"She's saying what are you gonna do about it, bruh," said the one who had not spoken the Russian word *dengi*, money. The other one watched her for a moment, trying to hear her thoughts. He took out a pocketknife, like the Soviet Pioneers would have. He said *money* in Russian again.

She raised her chin, sniffed the air around them. "This a lot of information." She squared up with them. "I can speak English. I do not have shit. If you want to do something, do this. You probably win. But it will not be beautiful. It will be very ugly," she said. The one who spoke the Russian word made a face like the scrape of a violin. From what she could see, the other did something similar, the scrape of a violin that drowned out the sound of him shitting his pants. "You not believe me?" Zina shrieked and moved toward them. They backed away from her, turned, and headed in the direction they had been going. They forced themselves to maintain the same casual gait as before the encounter. She stood there for a while as if on captured territory.

It had been too easy to cheat the American dream. Through some bureaucratic error, the kind that might have cost somebody their life in the Soviet Union, she had escaped deportation for participating in a protest and being arrested. They had not discovered her Ukrainian nationality. Usually bureaucratic mishaps were at best a massive fine, at worst a black sack over the head. In this case, she had gained from it, at least for the time being. Nonetheless, back in Detroit, she had not forgotten that her days were numbered in America. Valya had. They had even celebrated. And since it had happened in December, they had celebrated on Christmas, the American holiday. She had never celebrated Christmas, only New Years, the most important holiday to those of the Soviet world. That Christmas, 2013, she had made Valya celebrate as if it would be his last. He sat on the floor where the tree would have been. He said crinkled gift wrap paper was the sound of capitalism. Her laughter filled the room with Christmas cheer, which she would describe as a slightly alcoholic, saccharine, piney scent, like gin. Valya asked her how to say "crumple," and she answered, *skomkat*, which he repeated throughout the apartment, dry and silent with winter, creaking wood, the world outside crumpled in the snow. That had been their Christmas, an accidental holiday.

NINE

VALYA

Everything had the air of being accidental here. There was nothing official. All institutions and social infrastructure were, at best, well-intentioned. It would scare an average American. I refused to let it scare me. Nonetheless, I was here.

I was speaking Russian. I had never been an official member of any nationality. I had never even been an average American. Maybe I never wanted to be, but now I was breathing the air here. The air was moving in and out of my throat, and on it were Russian sounds, sounds that meant nothing to an American. Any meaning would be accidental. That nothing to an American was everything here. And America was nothing here.

Nonetheless, leaving the apartment, even leaving the bed, was complicated. I expected Zina's father to kick me out soon. His presence was constant, announced by his frequently clearing his throat. I spoke to Zina in jagged whispers as if we lived in a totalitarian regime, where and when the walls listened, and not in contemporary Ukraine. These walls, painted a pale white color, heard and said nothing.

Then there was a change in the atmosphere between Zina and her father. At the kitchen table one day, he suggested she work as a *krayeved*, a tour guide in Odessa. After all we had been through, Zina would become a guide for tourists of her city, what I had tried and failed to be for her in Detroit.

In response to her father's suggestion that she get a job, Zina stood and pushed her chair under the table. As she retreated, his mouth smacked open—and shut. He turned to me and said that he was sorry but there were no more eggs. I took the hint and stepped out to buy them.

I couldn't trust that his tolerance of me would last much longer. I needed to set out and find an occupation of some kind. My pocket dictionary was falling apart after a third re-taping. I only used it in secret. On my list of required vocabulary were *deposit, beer, cigarettes.*

At the store, when I used the diminutive word *yaichko*—egg, yes, and also testicle—the cashier laughed so hard she had to step into the little office behind the counter. She turned around in there and stepped out again, took a deep breath, and asked, *You buying for yourself?* The laugh, deep and raspy from cigarette smoke, opened her mouth like an old fashioned bear trap. Her teeth looked like they were pointed.

Abramovich tells a foreigner—whose Russian is a second language—a joke, something about a monkey. The joke's told in Russian, of course. The foreigner doesn't laugh. He tries so hard, asks Abramovich to repeat it several times. He memorizes the joke *word-for-word*. He ventures out in Odessa, goes to a kiosk, takes a gentle seat on a warped picnic table. *Have you heard Abramovich's joke about the monkey?* he asks with a sober face. His drinking companion shrugs the Odessan way, saying *I don't know* with his mouth closed. The foreigner retells the joke *word-for-word*. His companion chuckles, guffaws even. The joke worked, having gone through the foreigner's mind without catching.

When I told him about the eggs, Zina's father stared at me without even a sigh of laughter. *You bought them for yourself?* Meanwhile, Zina stared out the window. She had tied fake flowers in her hair. It made her more girlish. The tail of hair, wrapped around the plastic stem many times, suggested a repetitive motion done while she hummed. She raised her hands and fondled the slapdash braid. It was up to me to acknowledge what he'd said. I'd have to try to tell a joke in Russian. Somebody must have told me once that it's all about the set up. *You were never in America?* I asked.

Zina hmed and turned to her father, who sighed. She let go of her hair.

He explained, *After the Navy, I was on a research group made up of scientists from here, Canada, Great Britain, and the USA. But that came to an end after the vote to leave the USSR. I never talked with the Americans.* The fake flowers trembled when Zina shuddered. She stood and took a bowl with boiled potatoes from the counter to the table.

And you don't want to go to America? I asked. One potato protruded from the bowl as if pontificating about where it had been.

Zina said, "You won't make him go to America. He would die first." *Right, papa? You would die before you went to America.*

His fork clattered to the floor. He didn't move. *I don't want to,* he said, finally.

Zina forked a potato, brought it to her mouth, and bit in. While she was chewing, she said, *Because mama's there.*

He slammed against the table and stood. His was a tiny tremble as if the vertebrae in his neck were disintegrating. Zina continued to chew, turned her chin and made faces as if she was truly enjoying the potato. Her father's breath counted the seconds.

It was my chance. I took a potato from the bowl with my hands and put it to my mouth like I was playing a flute. I said, *This is how "Yankee Doodle" eats. As if I'm eating corn. Only we Americans know how.* The only sounds in the room were my gushing, exaggerated bites.

Zina was the first one to break the silence. *Pop, how do you say "pryanyi" in English?* She immediately shook her head, dropping this idea. *Well, whom am I asking? You don't know.* Her smile suggested cackling. Her father left the room. "Yummy," she said. "I think you would say 'spicy.'"

What was spicy, or "*pryanye,*" in Odessa were chestnuts. Such trees lined many streets, including *Seaside Boulevard.* I had needed to escape the tense, harsh moments in the kitchen with Zina's father. He would never accept me until I was like a local. I decided to walk without aim. That was the best way to appear to be a native. I wouldn't take a map, wouldn't consult any text about my path. The place, the street, would have to be the only language I spoke. If I was to be a local, I needed to be bored by it all. In reality, however, I was rapt there. I wanted to watch it all the same way I could watch Zina for hours, eager to see every new movement, to hear every new sound.

I walked until I reached a park through which I cut over to *Gogol Street,* where two male statues, like Atlas, held up a globe. Their faded and cracked muscles spoke the same language as street art I had seen in Detroit, and this language had passed from the United States through me to Odessa without my understanding. A brunette, wearing heels, a tight, short dress, and long earrings, all of the same blue color, kissed one Atlas and ran her fingernail up his chest, while somebody with jet hair, wearing buckled shoes and a blue suit over a tank top, led her away by the elbow. He touched the other Atlas in the same way, took a look up and down the street, turned to me and put a finger to his mouth for a shush.

Further away a group was setting up to film the couple. She adjusted her dress. When she noticed me watching her, I said, *Excuse me.* She smiled back and asked me if I would like to be in their film. Zina's voice within me jumped to my throat and said, *No. Thank you.*

Zina had told me I said *thank you* and *excuse me* too much in Russian, that it marked me as a non-Odessan. "I feel like the outsider too," she had said, putting her hand against my heart. I had reached to put my hand against her chest, and she had shown me her shoulder. "You go for my boobs? I was just fucking with you." After a second, she released and said, "You will never know." After she said that, as she walked away, she put her arms up in the air, like she had been carrying an invisible weight, a female Atlas.

Approaching me was a young man who, while he spoke, pinched the air with all his fingertips together, making a small mouth shape. "Excuse me. Is this *Lanzheron?*"

I glared at him and shook my head. I should have shrugged, like an Odessan. "*Nyet,*" I said. *Where do you want to go?* I asked, projecting my voice across the broken pavement and dusty cracks.

"I don't speak Russian," he said. "*Ya no govori russa.*"

"Okay," I reassured him, "We can speak English."

"I am Italiano. I come here on the train. I must meet a woman on Lanzheron."

"Let's walk in this direction." The Italian turned, began to walk, stopped and continued when I did. He followed, thanking me over and over, treading with care the ruined city floor. A woman passed, her heels deftly dodging the cracks and holes below, her head staying still, her poise drawing the attention of both of us.

"Maybe this the woman I should meet," said the Italian.

"You don't know what she looks like?" I asked.

"She looks like that." He shook his head and sighed. "You speak good English. Where have you learned this good English?"

I mumbled, "I'm American."

"What?" the Italian shouted. "Why have you not said to me? Why have you said, 'We can speak English'? You don't speak Russian."

I raised my hand to try to turn down his volume. "I do."

Now the Italian was glaring. "Okay." He passed his eyes along the street, and we continued. "I have fear in this place. I was on the train. People outside throw rocks against the sides of the train." This he said as if he and I were spies, Westerners infiltrating the East. I remembered to shrug at this. The Italian stopped again. "How are you called?"

"Valentine," I said the Russian way.

"You are not American. Who are you?"

"Who are you?"

"Sapienza. What are you doing here?"

"I'm after a woman too," I said. I wondered if he was meeting a prostitute and wished I had kept quiet.

"Okay." Sapienza glanced up and did a double take. Above us, a sign said *Lanzheron Stairs*. We had come from a different intersecting street. "I memorize these letters. This is where I go now, my friend. Thank you for this help." And Sapienza walked out of my life.

I walked further, continuing the conversation in my mind, stuffing my fists, like two hidden microphones, in my coat pockets. I vowed again never to speak English, even if my own mother came to Odessa to speak to me.

I crossed Sabaneev Bridge, weighted with combination locks, many of them red. They were red because they were clicked into place there by people in love. With Zina, I wanted to click a lock closed on that bridge. Even though this was an impossible ambition, I was here now, and I had no other purpose or reason to do anything else. I tried to dwell on other thoughts. Sabaneev itself was as decrepit as any bridge in an American city. One day it would fall into the trench it spanned, bordered by small houses. All those relationships, represented by all those locks, would smash at the bottom of the trench. In that trench underneath, a man strode as if on a serious mission. His balled fists gave him away as a local. When I turned toward the center again, I saw somebody walking, glancing at architecture, a hiking backpack full over his shoulders. If I wanted to be from here, I needed to come up to this obvious outsider with fists ready.

On *Transfiguration Boulevard*, some locals had gathered. They all wore sailors' hats. They had been partying. One sailor saw another far down the street. The first threw his torso back as if he'd fall. Before he did, however, he reached his friend and balanced, drunkenly. The sailor's hat had the words *Black Sea Navy* printed on its band. I'd seen those hats for sale on tables alongside Odessan tchotchkes. The sailor mentioned *Baltic tea*, which Zina later told me was basically an eight ball, basically cocaine. A mother and a little boy, holding hands, turned and headed in the opposite direction from the drunken sailors. I remembered being in a military ship, a museum, with my father. I brushed the memory away and followed the mother and little boy. When they spoke, I heard the boy's elementary Russian like my own, the mother's measured words like Zina's responses to me, as patient and reticent as a chime.

I longed for that chime of Zina's voice, practiced for it. I spoke every digit of addresses. It seemed impossible for me to do otherwise. 5435 was *five four three five*, not fifty-four thirty-five.

When I said, *I like it*, Zina and her father thought I was saying, *I don't like it*. Zina would have to explain, "You got to pronounce the difference between letters *m* and *n* better. You talk weird."

At another meal, still eating potatoes, I said to Zina's father, *Maybe I could teach you how to eat corn.* The joke had not been funny before and wasn't funny now. He set his fork down and glanced at me as if I was the buzz of a mosquito in his ear. *You understand the joke, right? Corn is everywhere in America. They grow too much, and they must have laws, which say that people must eat corn. We eat a lot of corn.*

"High fructose corn syrup, *da?*" said Zina, showing the white kernels of her teeth.

Her father picked up his plate. *Time to cut the cabbage.*

You understand the joke, right? I asked.

I don't give a damn what's in America, Valya. Fuming, he came and lifted her plate.

I put my hand on it and said, *I can.*

You can what? he balked.

I carried the plate to the sink and saw the cabbage. *I'll cut the cabbage.*

Go ahead, said her father. He leaned over her chair. She shrugged. He said, *Go ahead, Valya.*

I took the knife, turned the cabbage on its side, and began to slice into the middle. I treated it the same way I would the cabbage of any nation.

Her father was speaking. *Once, I saw a man in the street, and he said he was my uncle. Odessans are so tricky.* He paused, said his daughter's name as if she weren't paying attention. He waited a bit, still and silent, before speaking again. *So, I guessed that next he would ask me to pay for his groceries. But instead, he shrieked, "Cursed Alexianu!" and ran away. I thought about that moment for the last forty years. I think he knew my papa. Valya! That's not how you cut cabbage!* He shouldered me and gently slipped the knife from my grip. *This is how we do it. My daughter won't eat it the way you were cutting it.*

That's how we do it in America, I said.

Then that's how you do it there, he said, leaning the cabbage for the last cut.

Her father was kind, even generous. All voices were supposed to thunder like his, all jokes needed his approval. His disapproval, gentle gestures, became mnemonic sonic booms that knocked his language into my head. My visa would run out and turn my experience here into tourism. Yet my long, rambling Russian sentences were beginning to make sense. I had stood, like a birdbath, on the corner and understood all. It was a point of no return. I was no longer a foreigner behind a wall of ignorance. I was a spy. I'd cracked the code, only it was all mundanity, no secret plans. They, speakers of this strange language, were human after all.

Zina came to the door and asked me if I wanted a smoke. Since her father wouldn't allow us to hotbox his apartment, that meant we would step outside into the courtyard. It was nighttime. I'd woken once in the middle of the night and looked down to that courtyard, where I saw skinheads lining up, hitting each other on the back and gulping from forty ounce bottles. I wouldn't even be able to stutter in front of them. But, as usual, I sucked it up and did what Zina suggested, the path of my life the answer to her dare. In the hallway, she began to speak Russian, *You must admit, it's nice how this is all one word in Russian, "zakurit."* I acknowledged this matter without opening my mouth. As we stepped outside to the empty courtyard, she said, *So, I have an interview here.*

Where? The question sounded like something dropped in a silent, tiled room, like the one at the end of Andrei Tarkovsky's *Stalker,* only drained of water.

It's called "The Echo Archive." They say they want an American perspective on their mission. It seems they think I'm, she waited, watching me. She waited a long time. Finally, I shrugged, and she said, *an American. They are looking for somebody with good enough English*

96

that she can translate their whole website. She glared at me. *And there are many rich Americans who will give money to such a project. I have* "I don't give the fuck" *approach. It's true.* "I don't give the fuck. See." She flicked her cigarette. "We should do something." She didn't stir. I said nothing, not even a morpheme. Yet I still disappointed her. *You know, when I applied for a visa into the USA, they asked me so many questions, as if I was a prostitute? I was offended.* The woman says, "Horror happens, even to beautiful people. Beauty demands sacrifice." *My papa never let me know about such things. He thought this was too much for a girl. Or for a woman,* she said as if to her father. While speaking, she had lit another cigarette but not offered one to me. I was afraid to say anything, since we were outside. I was afraid my Russian would give me away as an outsider, while if I simply sat there mute, I would blend in, be a local in the eyes of all those who could look down on us from their windows. They would see through me to the ground, where sparse grass grew among grit. "You not gonna say nothing?" she asked. She had been watching me. She stubbed the cigarette out and crossed her arms. Behind her I could see an elderly woman in the window. She was hanging clothes outside, and she'd probably heard Zina's English.

I don't understand, I said. I tried to slur as if drunk. Zina gave a nod of approval. *I don't understand what you want. What do you want from me?*

"*Ukh!*" Zina called out. The echo raised the hairs on my neck. "What a man! You think that gonna fool somebody here?"

I hopped down from the bench and headed for the stairwell back up to her father's apartment. *I must leave soon. You know why.*

"Oh, yes. I forget about visa. You can just go to Moldova or something. Stay there a couple days. Come back. It doesn't have to be bad." She hopped down and moved toward me the way a cat moves toward prey. "Just don't go to Transnistria. That where they cut off Americans' heads." Her smile gave off the glint of a knife in the darkness. There was the perfect amount of enough moonlight as if she'd planned to speak from that spot at that exact time of night.

As we climbed the stairwell back to her apartment, she ran her fingernails along the walls as if to take all of it, the building, *Big Fountain Street*, Odessa, maybe even Ukraine into her arms and hold it there. Not me.

Once she was in the apartment, I, like a butler, sprinkled the table with sunflower seeds for her. Without looking, she split them and ate the innards. I got out her laptop and started to look up *Arkhiv Ekho*. I read one of the testimonials out loud: *The Echo Archive preserves that which should not have been preserved, which should never have existed, which should never have taken place. There shouldn't have been personal records of the camps, of life in the Soviet Union, of the personal betrayals. This shouldn't have been.*

I said, "It sounds like an interesting job to me." Zina's father was right outside the door, so English was the only way to have privacy.

Moments and history that should not have been the way they were, but which ended up that way.

Zina began to shriek laughter. "That the best joke of all!" Her father poked his head in and shut the door again. The laughter was cranked to a high volume. No other sound had a chance.

I would never be able to speak to her while she drowned out all other sounds. Odessa had returned her to some trauma, deep within, as faint and inscrutable as her sleeping heartbeat. I thought I needed to hear her suffering, to translate it. For whom? There was nobody who didn't speak either English or Russian. Zina's language was attached to all that she'd left behind and to which she'd come back. My version of this language was a cheap tchotchke bought in the park. It was something for tourists, not beyond minor transactions, themselves reduced to absurdity by my misunderstanding—eggs or balls.

Voices threaded in and out of the bleak mist in which we floated. One caught hold. "In couple weeks is April First. *Yumorina.*

The day of fools. Us. We fools," she said. "My friend Annushka has a party." I waited for a wink and caterwaul laughter.

That means, probably, I should work on my Russian, "right?"

She didn't answer. That was all right. I was making things happen here. My language was enough to move forward with what was happening to me. If she had answered, her voice would have lifted me up. After her voice passed, I would have sunk again. At least I was still afloat here.

In the wavy window, I was reflected, shivering with the motion of Zina slamming doors behind me. The light switched off. A man in the courtyard, without a sound, waved at me.

TEN
ZINKA

The voice of American Zina, an unseen beast, said, Go there. Walk into the courtyard like you own it. Listen to me. I got no accent whatsoever, the voice said. I am a native too, like that old radish, Borya-or-Kostya, who has a wart on his hand.

As if Borya-or-Kostya, the old man in the courtyard, heard that inner voice, he hid the hand with the wart from view. He began to sing *Dark Night*, the Utesov song. She refused to allow this song to perch in her heart. This song wanted her to forgive the world for its failure to uphold truth. She stopped his song by asking, *Borya? Or Kostya?* The way he looked at her, she did not think it was either of them.

She was on her way to the trolley along *Big Fountain* to meet Dasha, a librarian from a place called *Arkhiv Ekho*. This librarian might offer Zina a job, money, maybe enough to buy something good for her papa, even if it was only a bottle of liquor. He had kept himself from any alcohol for months. Yet money went to Galya. She could tell her papa was feening from the way he crossed his arms, almost hugging himself, when Valinka brought in beer. Valinka had offered to share. Her papa behaved as if he had not heard. Still not that desperate, he would take her charity alone, nobody else's.

Dasha had wanted to meet Zina because of Zina's unique perspective from having lived some time in America. What she would not tell Dasha was that she did not belong to America, had no purchase on it, same as Galya, only Galya had found some way in through a proud American. Anyways, they were trying to sell their suffering to proud Americans, people who would "support the mission" of exposing the horrors that had happened to people during the Soviet period. Zina did have a unique perspective. And if she could *clean off* with some Americans' money, why shouldn't she?

In America, she had asked about a job at the Detroit Institute of Art, where an exhibit of the work of Auguste Rodin, sculptures and some drawings, had traveled from Philadelphia to Detroit as if for Zina herself. She remembered standing and staring at a drawing of Apollo, which Rodin had done, copying Michelangelo. Rodin's sculptures made of marble came from Europe, like she did. They were here now, on display for every passerby. They were exposed to the gazes of all people who walked through and paid admission, including her, who watched for long enough that a security guard walked up and asked if she needed any help. "Yes," she said. The security guard asked how he could help her. "You have job opening here in this museum?" He smiled at her, sized her up the way Linda would. Americans assume that everybody should want to make love with them.

The Americans had appropriated this art, appropriated these figures out of the life of Europe. She had circled the torso, come as close as the security guard—who watched her intently now—would allow. She noticed the rough surface of these sculptures, more than only the genitals or the nipples. She had examined the surface of the sculpture of Balzac. It had been like that of a choppy sea. And that sea was black. It had been clear to her that such a surface could never have come from America, where people were too healthy and cheery to be able to make something from any roughness they encountered in their lives.

That was what she would tell Dasha. That would be her unique perspective on Americans. Yes, she would tell Dasha that she had been to the museums of America, more telling about the culture than churches. Museums were places where people were on their best behavior, quiet, wondering, not so far from praying. In museums, the godless could pray.

She came to a bus stop, watched Odessans and Odessitkas board a bus, and thought of a joke from Mikhail Zhvanetsky, who referred to paying bus fare as "making a deposit." She did not laugh at this memory of a joke by Zhvanetsky, and she decided to walk given that she was early and needed time to think.

Walking across the Sabaneev Bridge made her think of Detroit, specifically the Delray neighborhood, where she had seen a man fishing. Valya had told her that it was known to be the poorest part of a very poor city. She had asked to go there. Standing along the bank, a man, who had identified himself as Smythe, "with a Y," had approached them. He said he lived by the river ever since he saw how much the government took from his paycheck. "What about during winter?" Valya had asked. "I have an excellent sleeping bag," Smythe replied. Smythe had continued to stare at them, his arms akimbo, crotch stuck out. He had given off the air of somebody prepared to make further proclamations. Valya had kept quiet long enough that Smythe had sighed through his nose and left them alone, to which Valya responded, "Whew!"

Would Valinka react in the same way to the wretched of Odessa? She passed an open door that led into a building which was empty except for a man watching a TV sitting on a crate. On the TV was a mystic healer whom Galya had once recommended for her when, as a teenager, she had experienced a series of headaches. *Relax*, the mystic healer said. *Close your eyes. Don't look at the screen, at what I'm doing. You don't know anything about that. Focus on yourself. Your organism and mine are together.*

Zina smiled and said against the thick, old glass, *What a charlatan!* The man watching the TV sat upright. He had shut his eyes. He grunted the way Valinka did when he was reading Marx or some other bullshit. Dasha, the woman interviewing her — she would have to remember to address her as Darya, of which Dasha was the diminutive — was probably a nerd, probably even interested in the West to a degree. Zina let the sounds of her own childhood become the sound of Dasha's too. A mama like Galya had probably also worried over Dasha, discussed the reiki movements and pushed her to straighten her back.

Your soul, the mystic healer said the word for soul, another feminine one in Russian, *listens to you. She feels you.* She watched his movements, which resembled work at an invisible switchboard in front of him, through which the viewer could look, if he wanted, to see the man arranging the viewer's energies through the TV screen. Those energies had arrived to the screen through the cable that brought the electricity into which the sound and sight of the mystic healer had been converted. This actual event had most likely taken place in Moscow. It was very likely this man was no longer alive, having been around since Zina's childhood. Yet these people still believed in the invisible switchboard he had set up between them. Language was an invisible switchboard, not a beast or anything natural at all, she decided. It was a machine. If this idea were an outfit, it would fit her better, since she had also believed, from childhood on, in the great holy unity of nature. A machine could have faults. The mystic healer said, *This will take a certain amount of time. Nobody knows how many seances you must watch. But it will pass. You will heal.*

People like her papa still believed and, more importantly, still hoped, no matter how stupid she herself thought it was.

The cafe on *Gogol Street* where Zina met Dasha was new. Zina was listening to Dasha, Darya, explain the mission of *Arkhiv Ekho*. She had explained herself, her couple of years at the International Humanitarian University Odessa. She was staring deep into the young woman's eyes. She might even call Darya a girl. Many men probably had. Zina interrupted her to yell out, "*Dye-vush-ka!*" to the waitress. Darya's stutter, after a long monologue of uninterrupted and clear explanation, betrayed her consideration that Zina's calling the waitress *Girl!* was an unfortunate, chauvinist leftover of a past era. Darya did not refer to working women as *girls*. When the waitress came, Zina asked her for a cognac. This request caused Darya to betray intrigue. This intrigue, instead of a misstep in her speech, was expressed as a flash of the eyes and a wry turn at the corner of her mouth.

Order you a cognac too? Zina asked.

"*Nyet. Nyet.*" *Not early for you?* Zina liked this push back. She could almost hear herself and Darya — Dasha at the point of this fantasy coming true — pushing one against the other.

I hear what you're saying. It's interesting, Zina said. Darya sat back and crossed her arms as if she still had more to say. *Only*, Zina gestured back at the exit, the street, which led down to the

Sabaneev Bridge, to the statue of Catherine the Great, to the Duke of Richelieu. *Odessa is only old things. People come here, and they go to the cemetery. I will make good money, better money,* she indicated, with her eyes, for Darya to take note, *if I drive people to the cemetery.*

No, you won't, Darya answered, scraping her chair across the vinyl floor.

Zina scooted her chair too. *You know the anecdote about the old women whom Abramovich drove to the cemetery. He picked up some others, made some stops, and the old women made many comments. Too many comments. "Will we end up in the cemetery today?" they impatiently asked Abramovich. "You'll end up there. You'll end up there," he said.*

Yes. I know this one.

It's difficult to translate, Zina explained. *You have the word, "popast." In English, it's hard to translate this to mean the same. The idea of falling.*

That would be your job, Zinaida, Darya said. *Your job would be to resurrect the memory of those who perished without acknowledgment and to do so for Anglophone users.*

But what if they don't care?

Darya sighed. She knocked against the table as if it were wood that housed spirits. She raised her head slowly, the way only an Odessitka would. *Try it. Try it out on an American. You still have contacts from there, right? Try to translate something and see how it affects them.*

Zina let the idea bounce around, shrugged a couple of times. The idea was like the little ball of dough from a fairy tale of every Soviet childhood. The little ball of dough sings a song and escapes everybody, except for the fox, who requests that the ball of dough sit on her nose. Zina let this idea sit on her nose and sing to her. She wanted Dasha to sit on her face and sing to her. At the end, the fox eats the little ball of dough.

The way she was sitting, Dasha's fishnet stockings were visible. She wasn't the most beautiful. She was dark, even a little bit of a hermit. Galya had once said, *The devil doesn't need a lot of beauty. A lot of boredom is enough.*

She was able to retain Dasha's attention for most of the afternoon. They walked past the Opera House, which Dasha had called the national theater, as was the fashion now. Here, Dasha explained, her grandfather had sat and tried to work out by ear on his violin the arrangements coming from there. *He often failed,* she said as if she had heard him fail. The cobblestones there clacked and threatened to twist Dasha's ankle, suspended above her pointed heel. Zina held her hand, and they descended the Lanzheron Steps.

She only let go when they had almost come to the foot of the stairs, and they both looked into a tunnel where women stood holding themselves from the cold. These were broken women, both Darya and she knew. That was most likely why the two of them stared for so long at the women as if searching and failing for a way to bring them out of that tunnel. They all wore heels, short and tight skirts, tight tops too, which exposed their belly buttons. They held themselves from the cold. One of the women saw her and Dasha, and the woman held a finger up to her lips. "Shhh," she said. When a man passed with quicker steps than theirs, the woman said, *Good afternoon. Are you waiting for somebody?* Zina heard Dasha's heel slip on the moss. She reached for her and grasped only air. The women in the tunnel were not even wearing pantyhose. Their legs twitched like pigs at the slaughterhouse. They laughed without opening their mouths so as not to show their little kernels of bad teeth, Zina knew. For that reason, the laugh could never come into sound, could never be a real laugh.

At Dasha's apartment, Zina moved to kiss her interviewer. Dasha moved back.

She watched Dasha climb the stairs walled in broken plaster, heard Dasha's heels on the dusty, soiled concrete. A door opened and shut. Had Zina mentioned she needed a place to live, no longer wanting to live with her papa? She shrugged. She had wanted the job. She shrugged. A violinist standing nearby, who played for tourists, began the same exact song he had played five minutes before. "*Kakaya poshlust*," she said. *Such tackiness.*

When she came home, Dasha had sent her an email. Like an American, Dasha had needed a machine to say simply that they would like to hire Zina for the job.

ELEVEN

Valya

've made mistakes in Russian. That's the only way to learn. I've learned a lot. Unable to remember the word for *fruit*, once I said, *I love the chocolate nipple*. I meant to say, *I love the chocolate with juice*.

Another bad day was when I needed a toothbrush. I had seen kiosks that had shaving cream, kiosks that had bird seed. I thought a kiosk attended by an attractive young woman must have had a toothbrush. I approached unprepared. When I came to her and she brightened up at my approach, I said *Do you have...* I had forgotten the word for brush. *Teeth?* I put an imaginary toothbrush in my mouth and used my tongue to push my cheek out sideways. She gasped at me, horrified, and shook her head. "No!" she said and slammed the shutter of the kiosk in closing it. Once I understood, shame sucked me to the ground. A crow there cawed and hopped around the corner as if on her way to tell other crows about my ridiculous mistake. If you still don't understand, face a mirror, ask your reflection if they have teeth, put an imaginary toothbrush in your mouth, push your cheek out with the imaginary toothbrush, and watch.

There was a day when I understood, and the meaning was so dark I wished I hadn't. While Zina and I were dodging across a street — *Cars only run over tourists,* she said, *never locals* — a car narrowly missed us and pulled over nearby. The back door opened, and a man stepped out and lit a cigarette. As we passed, he said, *Come here.* This command was in the singular imperative, only spoken to one of us, either me or Zina. He had ogled Zina as he said it. Inside the car were three other men. They all ogled her too.

There was a time when I understood, even though my very appearance suggested otherwise. On the way to the party on April First, *Yumorina*, a man across the street saw me and beelined to our side to shout, *Give me a cigarette!* I was not smoking, and there was nothing to indicate that I had any cigarettes on my person. When I shook my head and passed by him as casually as I could, a whiff of air brushed my temple. I continued walking even though I was sure he had punched near my head. I told Zina, and she remarked about how much easier it was to request a cigarette in Russian than in English. The feeling of being an outsider punched the air near my head too.

This punch happened on *Big Fountain Street* where Annushka's apartment was, where her party also took place. *Fountain* had the sweet fragrance of acacia trees, which lined the street like hostesses nonchalantly awaiting us. The apartment building had a sticky coat of pink paint. Zina said the panels—Italian or French, she couldn't remember—on the sides alone distinguished it from American ugliness. For this American ugliness, I assumed, she held me responsible, since I was still nothing more than an American to her even after I had come to her city, lived in her home, eaten her food, spoken her tongue.

I met her friend Dima at the party. He said he was ready to leave. Now he'd stay since Zina had arrived. When she introduced me, he cursed, *Fuck. Now we gotta speak English?* She told him I spoke Russian. He sniffed me. "This a lot of information," he said to me. "You are the 'warrior'?" he asked me. I said, *I don't know.* I meant that I didn't know what he meant by warrior.

He introduced me as the American at the party. After that, everybody bowed to me. My sweat had begun to drip on the floor.

At the sweaty party, I said to somebody, *I'm excited to be in Odessa.* I had looked up the word "excited" online. The word *vozbuzhdyonnyi* came up. *Vozbuzhdyonnyi* typically means sexually aroused. Instead of *I'm excited to be in Odessa*, I had said, *I'm horny to be in Odessa.*

After they laughed at me, I became conscious of the language around me, and the party became like the Russian version of a Robert Altman film. A man said, *Let's change the subject*, and waved his hand as if clearing a fart from the air. Another man said, *He's speaking French. It's time to go home.* A performance began in the living room. A man came out in traditional Russian costume and began to dance the *hopak*, the ankle-bobbing dance where the dancer kicks out the heels. A woman came out, her breasts clearly fake, her voice clearly deeper than her singing voice, which was in falsetto. The song was in a mixture of the Russian and Ukrainian languages, what Zina had called *surzhik*. The woman with fake breasts, with well-toned muscular shoulders and arms and tight, skinny hips, laid a basket at the feet of the man in traditional costume. He cried. He cried like no American cries. He cried with his whole body. The DJ, a man with a jolly beer belly, said, *I'm so fat*, using the word *"tolstaya"* as if he was female. On the wall was a painting of the famous kiss between Brezhnev and Honecker.

I remember at one point using a word that simply didn't translate. Zina began to make out with Annushka. It was a spectacle. It all started out with Zina holding a mirror up to Annushka. After the making out was over, I called Zina a "fauxmosexual," I suppose out of wishful thinking. She tried to punch me too. I ducked. She said, "After Linda fuck me, she said she spoil my pussy with her tribbing. You know what tribbing is?" I shook my head. "Then you shut the fuck up." When I asked what it was in Russian, I thought she would kill me.

Instead she abandoned me at the party where everybody had laughed at me, so I drank till vodka told me the shape of my stomach, to try to bring the inner Russian voice, the one that sounds flawless, out. It was impossible. Something came undone between my mind and my mouth. Somebody sang a song called *Dark Night*, and Zina reappeared, very serious. I realized that she was the kind of person who could lash out one moment and become your best friend the next. She came up to me and said, "This song best represents us. Utyosov sing it. You can fall in love singing this song. Love under pressure. Love during crisis. Love during the wars and death of this land over twentieth century. That song, in that faint light, while you try to read lips. You can fall in love with such a song."

After she said that, I looked deeply into her eyes, dark in the dark light, gaping into my own, and said back to her, *I wanted*. I used the feminine ending, said, *"Ya khotela."* I said, *"Menya,"* as if things only happened to me, as if I was always only an object, as if I had spoken the words I wanted Zina, who would use that feminine ending, to say about me.

Dima interrupted our moments to say, *All that's left of my father is my patronymic.*

To try to top such a great line, I tried to do the *hopak* for Zina. My pants split in the crotch seam, and my shirt split up the spine.

Seeing this tear, Zina said, *So friendly. I love you.* It wasn't Zina. It was a woman I didn't know. And she hadn't said, *So friendly. I love you.* She had said, *So friendly. I love the South.* She'd said, "*Tak druzholiubnoye. Ya liubliu yug.*" *Yug*, the South, sounded like you. She was not Zina, and she didn't love me. She loved the South, Odessa in the Russian-speaking world. I told her I loved her too. I tried to kiss her. The sound wave passed through her as nothing or, at most, very little, a slight vibration. That was all my language was, a whisper's crest on the scale of volume. Sure, I'd said the words. What they signified had come across in that small way. My words hadn't changed Zina. They hadn't changed anybody. I was talking only to myself.

The party began to sing in unison *By the Black Sea*, and it's during this song that somebody else kicked me out. The door swung open outward, a foreign way to me. Usually, doors to apartments swing inward. It shut, muting the sound of the party. A mark, like musical notation, was on the wall at the height of my head. It resembled marks by the floor, where people's shoes had scuffed the surface, as if somebody had scuffed the wall that high up, as if that somebody had been upside down — *legs on top*, as they say in Russian.

Outside the air was so much cooler than inside the apartment. Again I heard, *Give a cigarette.* I said back, *But I have no cigarettes.* When I said this, a lit cigarette fell from my mouth. I remembered I had bummed one at the party. The bummed cigarette went to the ground as gently as a feather. Time was slowing down. The man who wanted a cigarette bent with a grunt to pick it up. *A lighter?* he asked. His voice sounded like his teeth were either missing or filed down. *What's your name?* I asked.

He threw himself at me. With some unknown source of agility, I sidestepped him. I was moving again. Behind me, he said, *Vanya. I'm Vanya. Don't forget!*

A block away, I turned into an alley to pee. There I saw the words *ODESSA* in Cyrillic and SHARPS in English letters. I almost peed on the English letters. The jagged right angles of a black swastika were crossed out by red lines that looked like shoulder straps. I thought I heard somebody call me a *penis*.

Zina was wandering along the street and calling my name, and it was lovely. When I approached her, she lunged backward, and the stem of her heel broke.

I was overjoyed to help her walk home on one broken heel.

TWELVE

ZINAIDA

Zina invited Valinka to have a picnic by the grave of her grandma in Tairovsky Cemetery, the third largest in Ukraine. They flagged down a Volga, she sat shotgun, and soon the three-story buildings had turned into apartment towers before falling away to a road straddled by the yawning steppe. The open landscape surrounding Odessa remained always so peaceful, even in archival photographs of the slaughter of the Great Patriotic War. Zina packed lunch, toasted bread and feta cheese wrapped in tin foil. Bored, Valinka opened his window. Alyosha, the driver, said, *Don't*, and shrugged. Even though it had only been a shrug, a mere shrug, Zina knew that it was a threat as she counted the crows on the power lines striping the road. When she was small, she would hold her hand up as a long blade leveling everything they passed, a building that resembled a barracks, an outhouse, its door open, light peeking in.

"Remember the outhouse thing at Trumbulldome," Valinka reminded her.

"Our outhouses are better," she told him. The outhouse braced against the wind.

Alyosha explained how he hated both the new government and Russia. The separatists were losers. A quick shower came down while the sun shined on. Alyosha recited what sounded like an Abramovich anecdote: *Ukrainians say when the sun shines while it rains, it means the devil beats his wife.* His cell phone rang, and he answered, *Yes, my beloved. I can't talk.*

As they tooled up to the second gate into Tairovsky, she asked Alyosha to stop the car. There was the start of a dusty chartreuse gravel road. She waited as if listening. Unlike many parts of Odessa and Ukraine in general these days, there were no guards at Tairovsky. What was there to guard? She listened and listened. From the corner of her eye, she saw Alyosha making gestures at Valinka. She turned around in her seat and reached out to touch Valinka on his knee, a move she knew would capture his attention. *Go, dear, and buy grandma some flowers there.* She nodded toward other people's *grandmas* sheltering beneath a tin portico. Even from the car, the bouquets of larkspur, hollyhocks, and snapdragon were visible.

Valinka went and did what was asked of him while she remained mute in the car next to Alyosha. When Valinka returned, she asked how much he had paid. Alyosha laughed at the price. *They swindled you.*

She turned to face Alyosha. *Here they swindled him. In America, it's trifles.*

Why in America? Alyosha asked.

Instead of answering, she stared at him for a moment before she turned her body to face Valinka.

Valinka tried to explain, *I think they said "thirty-three." But then she saw me go for my wallet. Or maybe she saw my shoes. She didn't look me in the eyes. When I held out thirty-three hryven, she said, "Thirty-three? I said three hundred three."*

Alyosha grinned with his mouth open and watched her, waiting for commiseration. She did not give it to him. She continued to attend to Valinka. "Here is some penny tray advice. Get it? Take or leave?" Valinka had no Odessan response. She continued, "Take what you get in life. Everybody gets scammed. They rip off each in their own way."

As she led Valinka further into the cemetery, the women who had ripped him off began singing in high, nasal voices, more like keens than entertaining song. The singing voices carried the repetition of a melody. The women chanted, cut themselves off, began again. This wail demanded only silence. It was the same way the trees, branches, and leaves demanded silence. It was the same way the stone did. These natural objects, these women, they demanded very little from people. Silence was the least one could do.

The late morning sunlight ushered Zina and Valinka further. The grass and weeds growing out of her dead ancestors—and Valinka's, as far as he knew—appeared to shrink from the brightness. The air hummed, fated with rain. They moved on foot over the dusty crush toward the sea of graves. The ground sounded wrong to her. The keening of the women sounded as if it were becoming louder, coming closer. Valinka could not see her face as she plunged forward, sweat pouring down her cheeks. Her sobs could be written off as panting. They passed a grave with a metal picnic table. Valinka stepped over to it and flattened his body across the metal, which clanged underneath him. On his belly, he put his arms out as if he were a parachutist. He must have been trying to impress her, show that he could be as wild and irreverent as she.

Get the fuck off of there! she said in a whispered shriek. He obeyed, hopping up and standing before her. He glared at her as much as she at him. *What? You'll say something?* He bowed. *Come on*, she said.

There are several wells along the little roads of Tairovsky. These wells helped mourners orient themselves there. She lead them in the direction of the third well, from which she knew to go until the sixth row. Prisms of light sprung up from the gravel as if it vibrated with the unheard voices of the dead. Groaning black, ironwork gates partitioned some plots. Some were curtained by listing weeds, cross-stitched by mute choke vines. Her ears began to swell as if somebody was talking about her somewhere else. She could sense that, behind her, Valinka was avoiding the ancient shapes of black iron. She could hear his mind observe that, other than a few Jewish and fewer Muslim plots, it was mostly an Orthodox Christian cemetery. He was probably used to Catholic cemeteries. In Tairovsky, there were no Blessed Virgins, no mothers around to cry.

Once they turned at the third well, the path became a small snake of bald earth floor, tapped out in the otherwise grassy soil of the steppe. The speed at which they moved, the wind of the path, urged them along. It felt, to her, as if they were running away. During a previous visit, she had heard her papa speak to her grandma's grave. As if he thought the wind there would sweep his words away and she would not hear, he said, *Zinochka is so much like you, mama. She's the best thing I ever made in my life.* That was what magnetized the tears to the brink for her. She moved faster so that Valinka couldn't catch up and see her face, hear the little keens—same as those of the hags at the front of the cemetery—mixed in with her somewhat labored breathing.

When they reached the grave, instead of telling Valinka, she stood in profile to him. She said, *You can't continuously renew your visa. When you must leave, will you do like other Americans, other Westerners? After you leave, will you "ghost" me?*

"Ghost" you, he said. *I feel as if you "ghost" me every day.*

She used a reiki hand maneuver to dismiss that theme of conversation.

But he persisted. *I'll say no. But I know words are trifles, no matter how close they come to the truth.* While he was trying to speak profundities, a flabby fly heckled him from a point in the air above. She, the fly, lit off like the tail of a pen stroke.

Zina said, *The advice of Abramovich: in order to kill a fly aim behind her—all flies back up a couple steps before departure.*

I was trying to speak to you about truth, he said.

She took a bottle out of her bag and set it on the grave as if clinking with the stone.

We're here? he asked. *I should have carried the bag.*

With a shrug, she said, *You know who impresses me? There is a woman from Belarus, part Ukrainian. A Russian writer called her a "lesbian kike." She's not a Jew. And I've never heard about whether she ate pussy or not. I like what she does. She wrote about the nineties, about Afghanistan, about Chernobyl. But she writes using others' voices. Only she doesn't do it in the way others do. She writes based on recordings, done on a little cassette, probably. She edits them. But some of these voices of real people are incredible. Whether from her or the people she records, that's truth.* For truth, she used the word *istina*, instead of what Valinka had used, *pravda*.

What's the difference? he asked. *Is "istina" more spiritual, "pravda" is factual?*

Yes, probably, she answered. *There's a third too. "Khuistinavda."*

You don't have to explain that one, he said. "I got it. Dick truth."

"That one's for you," she said. Tears, sobs, they had fled from her eyes, from her entire face with a morbid grin and chuckle. Without taking her glance from him, she pointed, "This the grave of my grandma. She was the tough woman. She was quiet and very strict. Like my papa, she didn't know how to joke." At her paternal grandmother's deathbed, Zina had told the woman how she had a crush on one of her classmates. Baba Liza had told her that whether or not he liked her, everything would be all right. Only it hadn't been a he. It had been a she on whom Zina had a crush. Zina had not corrected Baba Liza, at whose grave she knelt now. "*Babushka*, I want to introduce you." *I want to introduce you. This one, he's my boyfriend. I have a boyfriend from America.*

The leaves rustled, dust slid in silence.

The silence was interrupted. "*Yelizaveta Tikhonovna Bondarenko*," *Thank you that you made Zina's father, and that he made her. I.* He stopped when she put her finger over her lips. She moved it to his lips and pressed.

"You...what a fucking joke," she said. "That's stupid." She turned to him, ready to say that she couldn't love him because he annoyed her, because they were so different, too different. Between she and Valinka were *two big differences.*

She picked up the bottle of *Bready Gift* and gulped from the neck, long and slick, slopped her hand across her lips, and made as uncultivated a growl and burp as she could. Even though this gesture was unpleasant, made her wince with the pinch of the vodka in her throat, she did it. She swallowed the vodka and with it all of Odessa, all of Ukraine, all of the Black Sea. It had the same stinging bitterness that stayed in the mouth, that burned itself into feeling, that sucked her dry and threatened throbbing pain in the future. She savored this feeling. The vodka said to her, *It could be worse. I taste good right now. It's gonna get worse. So drink up, pal.* If she spoke what she wanted, acted the way somebody between the two continents where she had lived would, she would cry. If there was anything her grandma taught her, it was never to give a centimeter. She and Valinka were two different waves of the Black Sea. "Papa said this place was perfect for his mama. She loved the garden. It is the garden of people here." She narrowed her eyes. "It's probably exactly like gardens in America." When he inhaled to speak, she said, "Don't say it's not. It is. It's all the same."

It's all the same, he said. Of course, it did not sound the same.

THIRTEEN

VALINKA

needed to renew my visa soon. I planned to do so by leaving and reentering the country. Or I could simply return to the States, end this. It felt hopeless. Speaking Russian and living in Odessa had given me, a righty, the feeling of doing everything with my left hand. I'd heard that using the non-dominant hand was good for the brain. God knows whether that was true. I didn't feel like speaking Russian and living in Odessa had done anything for my brain or any part of me.

In such a state, I retreated to the beach to drink beer and stare at the sea. Fewer people would say anything about this behavior of mine in Odessa than if I were to drink by a body of water in the United States. Yet I was beginning to realize that the U.S. was home.

I was pondering the word Odessitka—after so many utterings, I heard only the middle couple of syllables, de-ceit—when Zina blocked the sun over me. She immediately took charge by stripping down to a bikini.

There was only one other person out there, an old man with a metal detector. I followed Zina into the water. It was cold, my nipples gave the signal. My whole body became as tight as a screaming throat. Zina led me until I couldn't touch the bottom. I swam behind her to the sea wall, on top of which she hoisted herself. When I clambered up and saw my feet on top of the wall, one of them was bleeding. Zina's clean, agile feet took two steps. She dove and swam further. I knew that I would go as far as she wished, all the way to Crimea. The beer wasn't helping me swim.

We spoke to each other, our tiniest mutters glistening across the waves. It was heavenly. I couldn't understand what she was saying to me. I was only sure that it wasn't what I wanted her to call out across the waves.

She emerged onto the beach again with very little splash. I watched her wiggle to pull her pants on, her toes moving the broken concrete like chess pieces. She squatted, her knees at the level of her shoulders, like folded wings. The smooth razor of the skin of her bare arms and shoulders would cut my touch. She avoided the debris piled in tiny cairns. This Odessitka moved as if she were swimming across the broken, bright concrete. I felt like the anthracite, pale amethyst, and sea shells embedded there.

A smell of flora both rotting and growing struck me, and I noticed my bag, which was strewn on the slab where I had sat. I hadn't left it, even to pee, until Zina arrived. Inside the bag, my wallet yawned open. The three hundred *hryven* that it had contained was now missing.

"Here it comes," Zina said. "Now you probably not gonna renew the visa."

Without having to think too much about it, I said, *How do you know*, here I hesitated before completing the question, *what I'll do?* Around us, people had begun to take notice of the couple who had swam in the Black Sea in April. One boy said, *They could take it.*

"I don't." Zina took stock of her surroundings. *You know what you'll do. Don't worry.*

"Thanks," I said. *Now I have no money.*

Zina crouched again in what appeared to be a perched position. There was something Eastern about this position. Americans didn't do that. At least, I didn't. *I think I know who took your money.*

"Who? You?"

She smirked. *Yes. I'm a thief, like all Odessans. Zhvanetsky says, "For us in Odessa, if it's quickly picked up, it doesn't count as having fallen."*

She tossed her arm at my strewn bag. *Maybe you shouldn't have left your bag.*

"You wanted to swim!" Loud voices meant there were ears to listen. There were certainly ears around us. The general din of the beach, echoed by the cliffs, became quieter. People waited to hear the onslaught in English by an American. I wouldn't give it to them. *Where's my money?* I thought Odessans would appreciate this question.

Zina had crossed her arms in front of herself. Even she didn't want this scene. She searched her surroundings before looking me straight in the eyes again, *Calm down. We'll find it.* She looked over my shoulder at the cliffs beyond as if somebody was escaping up the path there. *If I did take it, you would nonetheless still owe me. Let's go,* she said and headed in that direction. Again, I was following Zina.

After climbing the path, we headed down a road running along the coast toward the center of the city. Stucco resort towers resembled cruise ships lodged within the land and scratching at the horizon. "Apartments for rich people. Or for rich Russian tourists," Zina explained. "But now, because of Maidan, they probably don't come." Unlike the resort buildings, whatever was left of Communism was muffled by the foliage of the hillside, flexing and bending with the wind. These buildings, like her father's, came into sight erect and dark against the sky. "If they were Communist buildings, you would call them projects, like where blacks live in America. That's Communism. Projects." We had turned into a dirt alley, where the empty body of a car sat against a wall. Zina said, "*Zhiguli.*" Above an arrow were the Cyrillic letters ТУПИК.

"*Tupik?*" I read.

"Dead end," said Zina. She pirouetted in the light gravel. The motion turned up dust around her, like the magical dirt cloud of a Black Sea genie. She held out her arms as if to embrace me. "You should not feel too strong for this place. She will eat out your heart." She took off down the narrow alley labeled *dead end* into what resembled a yard. A bedspring lay there, next to it an axle with two large tractor wheels attached. There were farming implements. Objects were arranged so a stranger might wander in and impale himself. In one place, a bust of Lenin stood above barbs and spikes. Vladimir Ilyich's mouth was gagged by a tall weed that had, in its growth, navigated the unused machinery and statues to reclaim the place. Smells of rust and weeds laced the air. A small shack with a corrugated roof stood on wooden pillars, the door new and shining, the unfinished windows newer and sturdy, at least in appearance. There were traces of fire damage at one end of the house, and a kettle was screaming. "*Chainik,*" I said.

"*Da, da. Chainik,*" Zina said. "You gonna talk to this man? He will kill you. He has connections. He is not nice man. He come from the long line of thieves. His grandfather was famous horse thief. You really want your money back? You better leave him alone. Don't worry about money."

How will I pay you back?

She shrugged, laughed out of the crest of a smile made at the corner of her mouth. When she'd finished pitching her gaze out across Odessa, taken a breath, and looked at me again, she said, "You better not let him know you a foreigner. He hates foreigners most of all."

This would be a test. I became as stony and unchanged as the bust of Lenin. The door opened. A creaking, gaunt old man stepped onto the porch. He was drying his hands with a dirty towel. *What you want?*

Greetings, Volodya. Zina stared at him, her hands on her hips.

Who are you? said Volodya, not making eye contact with Zina, only staring at me. The older man picked up a large piece of rusted metal, tottered in place, and carried it along the porch toward a blank spot on the lawn.

I'm the daughter of Oleg Bondarenko. You and I are acquainted.

Ah, yes. The little girl who wanted to be a sailor like her papa.

Zina nodded. One at a time, Volodya moved three pieces of what could have been a jet engine, for all I knew. Each piece was larger than the last. Then he reentered the house.

Zina turned to me and groaned, "You gonna go in there?"

Volodya came out onto the porch again, and I blurted, *hello*.

The perpetual and fluid motion of the old man came to an abrupt stop. He bent, grunted, and heaved what looked like an engine block. It made a low, solid arc from the porch to almost within a meter of me. That was how I learned to judge a meter. Without that meter, I would have been crushed like the sparsely grassed soil mashed beneath the tangible sound of the object landing. *Where you from?* he asked, hands on his hidebound hips, head cocked to one side.

He's from the North, Zina slurred. Was it a joke? What's south of Odessa? Zina would say, *The Black Sea*.

Why speak for him? He doesn't know Russian? She looked down at the jagged metal pieces of what Volodya had dismantled.

Yes, I'm foreign, I said as if I were beginning a speech. *I speak Russian*. When I said this, I used the Ukrainian *h*, hoping to pass as a Ukrainian.

What kind of shit are you talking? said Volodya. *Get the fuck out of here.* His fist balled, his stomach tightened within his open, button-up shirt. My voice rose from my throat, my tongue and lips moved. Nothing came out. Volodya bent at his waist and lifted another metal hunk. He chucked it against the other one, the sound like ships colliding. Earth near my foot caved in. I retreated one step. *Go!* Volodya shouted. I sprinted out of the yard into the alley.

Zina ran after me until we were out of earshot, stopped, put her palms on her knees, a mockery of exhaustion, and said, amidst caterwaul laughter, "What fucking pussies!" She stared out at the landscape again, as if for her cue, and slapped my shoulder. This slap was like a gunshot fired at the beginning of a race. She slapped me as if trying to find out whether I would follow. She would take me as far as she needed to lose me. It was what she had been trying to do since we first met. Only there were two Zinas: the one people saw and, most of all, heard; and there was the Zina who begged me to listen to her, who spoke in a girl's voice and swallowed her words so that they would stay deep down within her.

After walking in silence for a while, Zina blurted out, "I don't know where my mom is right now." The sea was nearby. I knew this without seeing, hearing, or even smelling it. We passed an abandoned playground in Park Shevchenko. Staged figures painted on wood with cutout faces, the kind of carnival attractions found in rural fairgrounds, stood in a small fenced area. Those with faces not cut out had maudlin masks, sloping, sighing eyes. Were these Odessan grotesques? Or would I have to dismantle my life enough to make such thousand-word sighs as these figures, slightly exaggerated caricatures of Odessans? Odessa's color was homey.

Zina interrupted my wandering with, "You remember Nine-Eleven. I remember my papa said, *Vremya prishlo*. It was bout time."

Even though I tried to muffle it, my memory, located in the Midwest, told its Nine-Eleven story. By that point in the history of my family, my father slept on the couch most nights. Unemployed, he had no reason to leave the house. That morning, he was on the phone. The TV blared. Mom was out avoiding his presence. His voice was sharp and high, like he wanted to jump out the window to escape. That was my plan, at least, if the whole house was about to explode along with what was happening on TV. Father said, "It'll be okay. They're gonna find the men who did this." I asked, "Weren't the people who did this in there?" He said, "Shut up. This is very serious." When I was sixteen, I watched film footage of that day. This time, I saw the edited scenes of people jumping from the building, their falls ending at the same time as if with the same sound, as bursts in the collapse. I heard the previously muted audio from whomever had filmed that canonized footage of the second airplane hitting. He cries out "Fuck!" when it hits. The cry, so impotent, sounds as if the dude's late and can't find his cellphone.

Eventually we left the park and came to a square, where I approached a store with windows displaying nonchalant, even apathetic advertisements for alcoholic beverages. Wind wheezed through the door when I entered. I followed a humming sound to a glowing refrigerator. *Open*, a voice creaked. I kept mum. *The beer's cold.* Two bottles clinked, clasped in my fingers. *Where to, comrade? I'm here.* A man, bald as a cymbal, with thick glasses, magnified his squint. *You don't look like you're from here.* *No*, I said. The old man wobbled on his stool, more than half his height. His gaze said to me that it wasn't my look he'd noticed. My gait said to him that I marched to a different drum. An internet phone call rang from a back room, the only source of light for the room in which he and I were conversing now. Through that doorway without a door I could see a small table, a chair, and a newspaper. Could his life be back there, waiting for calls to break the silence, flapping the newspaper, sipping tea? Perhaps the old man lit up a cigarette once in a while, punctuation in the long sit of his life.

The door opened. Zina said, "Dude, I gave you ten *hryven* for beer. Why you take so long?"

Your friend doesn't understand the music of our majestic Odessa, said the old man.

Of course not. He's a "pindose." By wit alone you won't understand Odessa, Zina said.

The old man sang, *Strange days, strange people*, as he rang me up.

Outside again, Zina raised a bottle to her mouth and pried the cap off with her teeth, drank half, and smacked her lips. We climbed stairs. I followed each of her steps over the maligned stones, glued together by mossy detritus. The stones came from underneath the city, she told me, dug out to build the catacombs, secret passageways that led all the way out to the suburbs of Odessa, to the sea as well. The base of the city was hollow, brought to the outside. The city revealed its innards, even put them to use, until they became upturned cobblestones to chuck at the enemy.

These words she said to me from two steps above, and I listened, a mewling dog. It was night, buffering everything. Activity was whispered, if sounded at all. Street light gave a groaning leer. At the Potemkin Steps, she made a ghostly descent, her long, thin legs as rickety as a turn-of-the-last-century baby carriage. In the distance were hotels on the pier jutting out from the foot of the stairs, industrial-sized fans jeering. That was where Americans were supposed to be. This subworld was empty, those hotels full. Everybody had run for them as if from a fire.

Not I, a voice cried out. It had come from a recessed doorway, where a boy was speaking to a girl, who darted to move around him. He pivoted to block her. *It's just that it's really sad when your favorite girl doesn't want to talk with you. You go crazy.* There was a scream. Splats of rain began to appear on the concrete. "I would not want to talk either," Zina said. She circled, searching all the windows in the courtyard. In one, a curtain sprung against the glass. We minded our business and retreated from the couple. Any other answer to this exchange would have felt inappropriate, American, like meddling.

A drop of rain drowned out my vision, the kind of drop that would make a ploop sound. Attached to one of the buildings walling the street, a door swung open with a metallic whistle. A thin boy without a shirt leaned out and glowered as if cursing us in his head. With a smoky exhale, he asked me alone, *You here for the restaurant? Come in.*

Down a few steps and through an open doorway, the cafeteria was clouded by smoke. Dim fluorescent bulbs droned above. An empty glass case groaned, refrigerating nothing. The cigarette on his lip, like a wagging finger, he asked me alone again, *What do you want?*

Well, Zina began, *give us dill soup, if you have it. And a bottle of vodka.*

He ran a glance of calculation up her body. *We don't have everything you want,* the boy answered.

What don't you have?

The boy flicked his cigarette toward the sink and grumbled, *Dill soup.*

Well, vodka alone, said Zina. She grasped the back of a wooden chair and arranged it to sit down. She said, "What you always wanted. Dinner without my father."

The skinny boy, who was polishing a tool behind the machine, gaped. "English? Good evening," he said.

Good evening to you. We speak Russian, basically. But we're sort of internationals. Where are you from?

I'm international too. From Nikolaev. I came here to start a "biznes." Summer tourists used to come here. But, generally, they don't speak English. Only Russian. A couple Ukrainians. He came toward us with a tray on which was set a bottle, a vodka called *Bready Gift. You can pay with dollars.* The bottle made a heavy sound. He slammed the glasses he'd brought too. Zina turned her head, squeezed the bottle open, and poured to the rim of the small highball glass. She pushed the glass toward me. The boy, watching us, said, *So. Russians who know English. Who know England. What about America? How do you talk to such people? They simply don't know life any differently. They think, that we're poor little ignorants. But we, thanks to the internet, know more than you. We can see what kind of life you have from bunches of sources, photographs, porno. We learn from childhood to envy, sometimes with white jealousy, sometimes with black. But go screw yourself. I got my piece. I don't give a fuck about your money, your things. The day will come. I live as I live. I should write a site about this? If I had a site, it would be written there, in English probably, that I get up every day at half of seven, drive a truck around the city. By noon I'm tired. Early evening, I already have more of a taste for booze. I'm not as bad as some. I just have my little drunk, which doesn't hurt anybody. Then I sleep, and the next day, again.*

Holidays mean more people. So. To me, they're not holidays, but even more work than other workdays. Normal workdays—those are my holidays. So, I live a blessed life. His facial expression when he finished speaking was not one of whom I would say, "*On zhil blagopoluchnoi zhiznyu,*" *he lived a blessed life.* Who was I to judge? He had spoken each sentence as if we would refuse to listen to the next. Having stared at us for a while in silence, he broke off to prepare God knows what behind the counter.

Zina mumbled, "Chatty, ah?" I headed for the bathroom to escape her sound.

There I tried to come up with my own monologue, like the boy's. In the mirror, I glared, wheels of fire encircling my eyes. What kind of encoded conversations had echoed in this small space? Shouldn't it be from the belly of the beast out of a yawping mouth? The space was quiet, the English word "quaint" came to mind. It occurred to me that the violence and crime that had taken place here had been nonetheless honest, unlike crime from the West, had been nonetheless subject to a code of secrecy enforced by thieves' honor. I'd never break through, even if I committed a crime.

When I came back to the table and sat, Zina, without breaking eye contact with me, reached into my pocket and took out my wallet. The bright color of the credit card given to me by my mother blinked in and out of my vision. Zina's had been the sleight of hand of a thief who looked me in the eyes when she robbed me. Anyways, I would never call her that word.

At first I thought I was buzzed. My next thought was that I was certain I was already drunk. Soon we were climbing steps, and I looked back and watched the boy rifling through stacks of money, shaking his head, every motion of his hand as quick as a blow.

On the street, we shouted to stop a Gypsy cab. Again, it was a *Zhiguli.* Zina told me, in English, to sit in the back, where children sit, where teenagers have sex, where criminals sit after drunken

129

revelry. Zina, in the front, would explain to the driver where to go. He asked if we were "coked up," his only English. When he eyed me in the back, she gestured at the road. The car sputtered along. Somehow my jeans had become tattered, worn threadbare in the pockets, with black grease markings here and there. My skin tingled with alcoholic heat rays. I wanted to curse at somebody, and I wore this readiness in my face, like the boy at the restaurant.

The driver moved the wheel as if he were taking something apart. After one quarter revolution, his hand moved to Zina's thigh. She shifted in her seat while the hand rested there for a moment before grabbing the wheel again. I mouthed unholy, empty oaths, what I would do to the driver once the drive was completed. On the dashboard a hidebound, thuggish Jesus repeated them.

About such an icon, Zina had once said, "Orthodox Jesus is the Jesus you don't want to fuck with."

When we arrived where Zina had directed him, the driver looked back at me, waited, and nodded when I said nothing and scooted over to step out. He raised his hands and shrugged as if to show that they had never touched money. Zina took my hand, held it tight, and whispered in my ear, "He pinch my butt when I step out," as if to amplify the anger which threatened to overcome me. She led me through a gate, heavy as railroad ties suspended in air. Rapid fire came from the distance, either a machine gun or pyrotechnics. Nearby was a Ferris wheel. Zina pulled me a couple steps and said, "You cannot stand in line?" Everything had tapered to a point of activity at my hairline. "You probably rode the devil wheel in America." We waited in line long enough for me to stand in a posture that marked me as an interloper, long enough for me to stop making dramatic sighs. When we stepped up to the Ferris wheel, my stomach sank again.

A metal bench flapped under our weight. The basket rocked uneasily, even while the wheel was stationary. The hinge connecting our lift strained, and Zina grinned as we ascended along a chain of small clicking links. I'd never heard the word for Ferris wheel, what Zina had translated into English, a *devil's wheel*. Of course, it sounded more sinister than "Ferris wheel." The edge of the metal bottom of the seat felt sharp enough to pierce the skin of a fat thigh. "What is it in English? Fairy wheel? You ride the fairy wheel in America?" Instead of answering, instead of uttering anything, I began to rock the car back and forth. Zina rocked with it. She exhaled, her grip splaying on the bar. She showed her teeth when she smiled again, more like a cat this time. The car grunted, squealed. Gravity lost hold for a quarter second, a half. My stomach sloshed, my limbs became the strings of a viol. "You gonna throw up?" Zina asked.

"No." Somebody below shouted at us. At the height of each swing, when the cab stopped with its floor almost vertical above us and the ground became visible, Russian filled my mind. *This way you'll die*, my Russian voice told me. As if in a centrifuge, this Russian sentence gushed through my brain and pressed against all senses. Our arc almost touched its apex. I was one clapper of the bell. The *devil's wheel* began to turn again, and slowly we lost the momentum we had gained, ticking faster toward death. Zina mimed me.

When we came back down to the platform, the operator stood guard. He had harmonized with our fear. He was touched. As we climbed out, he said, *Who raised you to be such fucking idiots?* I prayed drunk's prayers that Zina would take this to heart.

Instead, she answered the man with, *My parents are dead. So, maybe in the next life.*

How many lives had I lived, how many times died, since I had been in Odessa? Her hand was outstretched again, this time to flag down another car. I was the air she sliced, whose everyday flow she blocked. I took her hand in both of mine, raised it. Her glance hissed. *Please*, I said. *Not again.* Hearing the plea in my voice for once, she led me from the road.

Strolling again, we passed a large roundabout with a sickle and hammer monument.

She was leading me to a bench, a pond-sized puddle in front of it. Men, with bottles at their feet, sat on benches nearby. They listened to us. My mouth went cotton and made tiny splitting noises. Even Zina was mute until she whispered, "We need their drinks." My head wobbled to signal my dissent, the motion equivalent to a whimper. "*Oi, blyad*," she said, taking my wallet again and walking away.

I didn't look at the men. However, you can't not hear. They were speaking, speaking about me, about us. Their volume increased until one said, *He fucked her just now. That's why.* They all laughed. I chuckled, and they laughed even harder.

Zina returned with a plastic bag and took out a bottle to drink. She handed me the other one.

Hours passed as if swallowed, one gulp. There were hints of honeysuckle, which I found lolling on a nearby fence. I pinched one blossom and slurped its little nectar. One of the other drinkers began spasming. Was it fake? Nobody said a word about it. Nobody heard a word I said, no matter how loud or enunciated. If I started talking, a strange equation whisked several moments away.

We slouched there, never becoming comfortable, well into the morning, sometimes snoozing along the bench, sometimes upright and breathing, heaving air like we had dreamed of running, or drowning. Others sat down and saluted us. All names became drops of dew. Time bubbles echoed along the inside of my skin like mercury, changing direction so rapidly, the past and future were as equidistant as they were impossible. Alcohol alone was ever flowing.

I sprung awake on the bench. Afternoon. My wallet was still tucked in. I was alone with recently returned *nightingales and pigeons, who stuck around.* In my mind now, I have a memory of Zina speaking the Russian, saying, "*Solovyi i goluby, kotoriye ostalis.*" The Zina inside me says, "I watched over you. You weren't alone."

She wasn't there, though. Nonetheless, I believed I knew, like an invisible thread, the steps, pavements, and corridors to wherever Zina was. I made my way along, patting for my wallet a few more times as if I could rub it to determine its contents. One foot made a padding sound, as if bare. When I looked I saw a shoe on it. When I examined it more closely I saw that the sole had been cut out, like the faces on the figures in Park Shevchenko. There was a faint vibratory glow everywhere as if a fluorescent light were underneath it all. The world had the motion of a crooked violin. I entered a store and found Zina.

We left together, still in silence, and I took a bottle of beer from her bag. As I opened it and drank, a car came to a screeching halt meters from us, and a man exited howling. He ran toward a man who had been sitting. That man jumped to his feet and started running in escape. I thought of the word *nedolyot*, which means an undershot. The car door remained open, the light on. A beeping began, and it sounded like it would never stop. *Nedolyot* has such a feeling of failure attached to it. I think I remember Zina saying that *not-quite* was the right translation, when she was trying to explain my unrequited love for her.

It was after sundown for the second time since we had met on the beach. Instead of more vodka, I swallowed dead air. We had come to a different apartment building, not Oleg's. Nine stories tall, it was cracked and patched, with wooden panels dangling off balconies, loose barred windows clanging on the first floor. A boy hung from the bars of one window. His feet were anchored against the lower rungs. He hissed at me. Inside, a woman was mewling.

Through the vestibule and into an elevator, we moved in silence. The elevator's ascent sounded like sharpening a knife. When the doors opened again, Zina removed a set of keys from her pocket and said, "This where Dima lives, with his grandmother. He will have the vodka you want." I hadn't mentioned vodka for a long while. The door opened with the noise of fracturing wood. She strode into the hallway, turned left, left again, faster than I could follow. *Dima, you there?* After hearing no response, she said in a quieter voice, "I think he's asleep." I bumped into her. "Just like a fucking *Amerikose*. You still didn't learn to take off your shoes in a person's house. Barbarian." My fingers fumbled the laces. She deadbolted the door.

In the next room, the kitchen, a ghastly natural light came from a gasping window. A breeze passed through the tiny space into the hallway and carried with it the sound of children on the playground outside. *City of courtyards*, I thought. The awkwardness of how it sounded in my head made me think it must only work as an American sentiment, in English. My stockinged feet touched the aching, scored wood. There was a bottle of *Bready Gift* on the table, a minifridge on top of a counter that bowed enough to crack, an old deep sink, knives and spatulas and spoons on a magnet screwed to the wall, a sink full of dirty dishes, and a doorless cabinet with a pair of cups and a plate inside. Our echoes lead to ceilings high enough to make my head spin. The floor was made of scraps of wood placed in various combinations, a warped and splintering game of Tetris.

Zina poured, leaned against the counter, and told about a man who always stole from people. One day the man raised an axe so high he blocked his ear on that side. The would-be victim only stood there, not defending himself, making a face as if he didn't hear Gabriel's horn. Zina herself, who at the time had been waiting for the trolley nearby, took the axe wielder's arm down through clear air. She had seen human evil, cracks where life slipped through and survived, ragged, after the apocalypse had come and gone, failing to deliver rapture.

I still hadn't reached the end of the bottle of *Bready Gift*—one quarter left. "What you think about our *zapoi, Amerikose*?" With this last word, Zina pronounced the first e like a Russian one, like the e in the three-Cyrillic-letter word *nyet*. That meant her tongue had arched up to touch the palate, like a figure rising up in prayer and bowing down again to touch the ground, submitting to some ornery Orthodox god, who has ordered him—since the tongue is masculine in Russian—to bow down. My tongue was passed out waiting at the tail end of a headless, snaking line of slurring voices. This hanging out would end badly.

When I came to, Zina was close, fumbling with my arms, crossed in front of me. They twisted behind the back of the chair. I was able to resist. Something was forcing its way into my mouth. The bottle of *Bready Gift* kissed my lips and sloshed forth. The sound came over me like a blackout wave.

The next time, the tea kettle's scream woke me. Dima's grandmother waddled into the room, her slippered feet shuffling along the floor. I pushed myself up from the table and bowed my head to her, my hand over my heart. There was a very slight possibility that, if I hadn't been drunk, the gesture might have appeared genuine in its respect. She tossed her frail hand toward me. Zina saw this exchange and said, "His *babushka* don't talk much. When his papa left, it cause her lot of pain. And she has lots of health problems. We must take care of her."

The grandmother was filling up the kettle again. Without looking at me she said, *Sit, sit. Zinochka will give dinner.* She herself stood, waddled out of the room, and came back with a photo album.

Zina explained, "You know how Russian hospitality is, Valinka. You can't refuse."

My knuckles mashed the table. The grandma was talking, showing pictures of herself and boy Dima. In some she was topless. Like a scholar, I analyzed the photos with her naked breasts, round and smooth and older than I would ever be. I yawned, and she shut the album. Her gaze had volleyed between Zina and me. She huffed and said, *He's a good boy, my Dmitry. He has good friends. I know that Zina can be tough. Don't be offended, dear.* The table wobbled under my weight. The grandmother set one elbow on her knee, her chin in her palm. When I looked at her, she sat upright, and I was ashamed that my gaze had caused this. Zina busied herself, taking out food already prepared and putting it in the oven to warm up.

We ate, or, at least, I did. Zina screwed the cap onto the bottle of *Bready Gift* until it gave a smeared-out whimper. She cleared the table and shrugged, all business.

We left the apartment and kept silent as we wandered again, this time along *Big Fountain Boulevard*. I distracted myself, snorted, pretended to notice the people moving along the streets, sloping down. I listened to the signals put out by those people, dressed in luminescent static clothes and scaly buckled shoes. From a dark street a woman emerged and asked me if this street was the way to the club *"Chistilishche,"* which Zina later explained meant *Purgatory*. Zina didn't remember hearing this, and she wondered if I had read it somewhere and simply made it up as the name of a club. I remember giving a shrug and saying, *"Da."* Zina stayed silent.

A car came at me without slowing. I dodged right in time, didn't look back. We turned a corner and were swept up in a herd of people moving toward a pool. This place was the club, over the door of which was written, *This is only the beginning.* The crowd was bodies in my periphery, unheard, unified and apart from me. I had been the one to tell the woman where the club was. I had been the one to stand up from the bench and go to the place where Zina had set the vodka, far away from me, take it back to where I'd slumped, and pour. I heard pour in Russian, the way Zina would say it, in three distinct syllables — *na-li-vat*. The beat drew me forward like undertow. For an instant I focused on a man standing sentinel in a dark corner, his shirt so tight his nipples showed. The man grinned at me with small, widely spaced teeth, like the stamps at the end of typewriter levers. Sound punched the air, showing itself in pulsing wisps of cigarette smoke, until I realized the wisps were people too. At a table nearby, men were drinking with their arms linked, *na brudershaft*. Zina would explain that the latter word of this phrase is German put to better use in Russian. After they shot their drinks, the men flicked the glasses to the floor. I waited for the sound of shattering. Everything was shattering, all at once. Nothing was whole. A man in a light suit was slumping, his legs spread like a taunt, knees guarding two women, who sat with their purses covering their hands as if they were cuffed to the table underneath. The man cocked his head to the side, his shoulders swelled beneath his jacket, threatening to burst the seams. On his t-shirt was a cobra backed by its hood. He and I came close, struggling with our arms, our feet sticking to the floor. We were dancing. We were brawling. The man made a fist, and I closed my eyes and waited for it to stop itself with my face or my gut. I swam around him. Others wrestled on the dance floor. One man danced around them as if that was all he had come to do and he would never stop. Flailing arms whipped past, the backs of palms felt soft womanly tissue, fingertips tapped hard and tight denim. Zina would say, You had to grab onto somebody who would drown before you would. Hold the foot that kicks you, if you're unmoored. Zina herself had jumped up and wrapped her legs around my hips. I held her up, twirled her while she shrieked.

The spinning center drained, and she dismounted. In the dispersal of the crowd, I lost her and came outside again. I felt cursed to wander the streets, separated from Zina. I wanted no longer to be drunk. People, trees, all passed me like the noise of ghosts in bloom. A group of young men sat at a bench, leaning with elbows rested on their knees. Dice rattled across the sidewalk. *Give the American the bones*, a voice said. I guessed, correctly, that the word bones meant dice. "*Nyet. Nyet!*" *Go fuck yourself, American. Quick. You're in the way. Go!* He stood. *Fuck, why do we play here? Tourists, foreigners...*I wandered away, repeating these words in a whisper. Down below, my pants had ripped open almost to the crotch.

By another group of people, I asked, *What are you doing?* One of them detached from the group and said, *We're doing meditation. Why here? Why now? Because here, now, in these circumstances, with all these sounds, there's more possibility to become distracted than anywhere else. We're testing ourselves.* He sat and shut his eyes again.

I passed more clubs, more people enjoying one another's company. Ahead were picnic tables, a kiosk. I felt inside my pocket and found a paper bill, five *hryven*. Zina would say, *If life's within, drink and die.* It was an old sailors' saying, something she had heard her father sing. I bought one more beer. Rotten fruit had spilled onto the street and spoiled there. Birds were eating it. Light lined the sky. The trees in the wind sounded like the broken waves of the Black Sea sizzling out. A man wearing pseudo-military gear shuffled from the shadow of the rustling plane trees, leaped from a ledge.

Zina, like the angel of death, came upon me. She was singing another raunchy couplet, her voice deep, aping a male's, *Last night I boozed so much, my noggin hurts without mercy/ If you're an honest man, you'll kill me, all right?* We passed a sign for *Transfiguration Street*. I no longer wanted to throw up, and the feeling was like trespassing in paradise. A small, empty square opened before us. Growing out of the cracks, weeds stood sentinel. As the light grew, bodies of those sleeping in the park became visible on all the benches, each covered up by cloth or newspaper.

We came to a wall, where Zina climbed to the top. I looked down at my fingers, swollen, thudding together. Judging by the lack of pain, I didn't think they were broken. An oily stain wrapped itself around a middle knuckle. I reached up to climb. My stomach flipped. Again I knew how my splatter would sound. Zina's touch helped me stay astride. She dropped from the abysmal height into the courtyard behind the wall. The shadowy bottom of the fall kept me balanced, sharpened the connections between my vertebrae. I swallowed what had come up. Soil emerged from the broken asphalt. Zina held her hand open, and I understood this sign meant I should stay quiet.

Around the side of the building, a placard read *First City (Jewish) Hospital*. Zina had taken my hand again, and her grip felt as if it withheld the flow of my heart. Against the wall were piled bricks and broken pieces. When we came close enough in the faint, rising light, a dark spot on the ground turned out to be a hole. Zina whispered, *This is a pit into the catacombs.*

Our steps inside that space fell on a wet and slippery floor. I walked ahead of her, too confident now that my language would lead me. Before I saw it, an abyss opened beneath me and I pitched forward, slamming against the rock. I tasted dust on my lip, split, I could tell, because I could also taste the pus that oozed there. With my eyes closed it wasn't any darker than if they were open. I couldn't remember if I'd flipped, and I had lost track of which way was up. I spit, and it splattered my face. I scrambled to my feet and turned to run in the direction I had come. The direction from which I'd come was a hole above. The tunnel opened up enough that my steps echoed. A long, deep gouge along the wall guided me.

If I'd lost my hearing, my ears crushed by the rock, I would have been better off, because sound there was locked in stone. I pressed my cheek against the wall and heard what sounded like a panther's roar. I called Zina's name. Nobody was there to hear me cry. You thought, the Zina inside me says. Yes, I thought I was alone. The tears were like a small underground stream no human knows, burrowing its way through the world. My mother appeared in the darkness before me. She was folding my child-hood quilt. This obvious delusion was the beginning of some-thing the name of which I wouldn't say, at least not in English. In my mind, only Zina could say it. Her voice said, In Russian it's *smert*. I can say it in English too—death.

I would disintegrate into the stone and flow into the world's depths. The matches from the club were in my pocket, which pressed against the wall. I took them out and counted with my fingertip—eleven. I struck one. On the wall, I read what I would translate as:

> *In the damp catacombs deep*
> *where it's hot and air's thin*
> *but the width here saves us*
> *think space, not death, to win.*

There were no bones around me. Who wrote this must have exited. I decided to move forward.

I crawled through a small tunnel that became narrower. I thought I would have to go back. The past was solid stone wall. I thrust and twisted until my bones should have cracked. I let out all my air. I gave up on the next breath. Suddenly I popped out. It was a large room. For a few minutes, all I could do was shriek. My shrieks reflected off the walls and divebombed me. This glorious noise kept me from shivering to pieces. After that, I could be silent for a while, lighting a couple matches, not trying to rub myself into the wall and floor. I peed into one recess, the whole time reassuring myself that people made these catacombs. Somebody had seen this place before. The walls had known human voices. I lit another match and read, in French, LES PROLETAIRES DE TOUT LE IVOND UNISSEZ. Even Zina's French was better than mine, and she would explain to me that a piece of the M in MOND had been rubbed off.

I heard a splash of water, so I lit the seventh-to-last match. There was a pool of albino fish, about the size of river bass. If they could survive here, I could. One fish had beached on the pool floor because it was so big. It finned the surface, splashing the silence, as if it were trying to purge. Before the match burned out, I saw the square, carved dimensions of the cave. Otherwise it was pure, unhewn rock. The splashing of the fish continued. The pool spread its sound out like a web over all.

A sound like a crashed hi-hat, muffled at the end, said, *Go in the direction of my voice. Follow me.* I fumbled for my matches and dropped them. As I clawed at the floor, the voice said, *What are you doing?* This person and I were already informal. The echo amplified the voice's quaver.

Who are you? I said, the *you* formal.

It's Zina. You don't recognize my voice?

No. I didn't believe the voice. It sounded like a girl's. Zina wasn't a girl.

I said, *If it is you, I'm here. I fell into this trap.*

I'm sorry, the voice said. If it was Zina, this apology would be her only ever. *But the whole world's a trap, Valinka.* The *whole-world's-a-trap* vibrated from the layered rock of the walls. *Go three steps to the left*, she said. Again I was supposed to follow her voice.

I asked, *How do you know where I'm located? There's no light.*

I know Odessa like I know myself—from underneath and inside. The voice laughed at its own joke, more behavior very unlike Zina's. *By sound, I can figure it out quite well. So, three or four steps. I don't know how long your steps are. Let's say, go until you come up against the wall. Then turn left and touch the statue there.* I did as the voice said. *You know, there's artwork down here. When they were digging, they made statues out of the material.* When my step struck the wall, I turned left and reached up with my hands, palms listing outward. *Odessans built their city out of itself, out of its ground, the shellrock.* My fingertips tapped stone, and my palms kneaded the surface. It was unlike the craggy floor and the indented, rumpled walls along which I had run my hand. *The catacombs are what's left.* It was smooth stone I was nestling, like taut cloth, like the voice. I slid my hand upward. *From here all the houses in Odessa come.* I reached a point where the curve of the stone changed, and I slowed the drag of my chalked fingertips. *But Odessans forget the catacombs.* Long, smooth stone led my hand to the next crevice. I couldn't reach higher. At the base the floor rose, elevating me. I kept one hand on the middle section of the statue, which bulbed out as my fingers traced toward the ceiling. *How can they forget from whence they come? How can they forget what has made their dreams come true? Do you feel her breast?* The spherical stone drew my hand inward. I lost my footing, and my face pressed the statue's abdomen, my lips mushed against the stone.

You already told me that, about the city out of itself. I'm touching her. Wow, I said.

Yes. Very nice. They preserve this here, under the earth. For what light? Zina would remind me that the word she used for light here might also have meant world.

Very beautiful. But why is she here? Is this a metaphor for death?

Zina's voice sounded even further away. *What does it mean? It means that you must keep your desires secret. Underground. You must never let anybody know. That's how they can hurt you. Well, what. You have a lot of questions. I can't answer them all.* Her voice came closer. She touched me, put her hands on me and embraced me. She kissed me, our tongues intertwined. We dropped to the floor, my knees hitting the cold stone. She was cold too. I was cold. I fumbled with the buttons of my pants while she ran her hands up and down the sides of my body. Her voice had reclaimed some of its cynical depth. *You want me.*

I struggled with my pants, removed them to my knees. She did the same. *I always wanted you.*

Maybe I can want you too, she said. She kissed me again, and we lay on the floor. I felt her pelvis, and it crushed and turned against me, threatening to tear me off. *This is what you always wanted*, she said. *I want what you want.*

I had become so used to her dismissal of me, her refusal to recognize my experience as one that mattered. I even worried that I wouldn't want this new Zina who wanted me. "*Da*," I said. "But let's stop talking. *Ne nado.*" She pressed me against the stone. I remembered how this phrase *ne nado* had affected her before. She breathed across my ear, and it sounded as if the entire catacombs breathed. *Ne nado* was a common phrase in Russian, one I still used consciously. She let out a howl, and the sound echoed off the cavernous ceiling as if she had rolled her head back, as if to crush me within her, never let me go. I wished I could see her face, see anything. What had happened was already more than I should have wished. My whole body and being aimed toward her through my center within her. I wished, and it was over.

I lay back and spread my arms. She sat up from me and said, "You got what you wanted."

I sat up and reached for her. *And you?* I asked. I found nothing of her in the dark.

I fuck you, and you still want more?

The air became clammy again. "Sorry," I said. There was the Zina I knew again. Even though I had come, even though I had experienced that which I had longed for, had given up on, I was glad that it was over. This Zina I could handle. I didn't know how long I'd survive the Zina who had made love to me.

Zina sighed, and it was as if the cool air and even the stone walls of the cave contracted. I said, *It's strange that you said this whole world is a trap. You're right.*

I was right? It can be a trap. It can also be a way into the bright, bright museum. You must go through the trap first. We're under the museum. Here you can exit onto the surface, if you want. A gust spread its wings over me. A light opened and brightened to illuminate a stair. I squinted as more lights slowly came on.

Where? Which museum? I asked. Faint opening light showed her, invited us upward.

By the time we reached the door at the top of the stairs, the pitch black cloak had swooped down again. I pushed the door, it opened, and I stepped out onto a tile floor. Zina shoved me aside and shut the door behind me. It slammed on the secret darkness.

On the opposite side, a sign next to the door read *Entrance Into Catacombs*. The wooden floors were also scored. Between sections were wide gaps. An old machine hissed and ticked. A gauge on it told some environmental factor, maybe humidity? High and low ceilings, like a series of upside-down locks along the canal of the hallway, defined the individual rooms. Through a doorway I could see a painting of an autumnal scene, a tree before a house that spoke of pre-Revolutionary Odessa.

Through the museum, older women came close, glared, and glanced back to check, their faces as wooden as the walls. There were more steps, guarded by dentilated pilasters. People had begun to whisper. A security guard shouted. A ticket taker yelled *Please!* "Eh! *Izvinite!* Excuse me, sir."

Outside Zina walked the perimeter of the courtyard, in its center a fountain. In the mirror made by the fountain's thin layer of water was an American covered in dust. There was a statue of a man and young boys grappling with a snake. A couple approached, and the man jumped up and put his arm around the struggling hero, his hand patting one of the boy's heads. The man threw his leg out, like a Rockette, and held the pose while the woman took his picture with a phone. People were seated, chatting and chewing outside, under clement weather.

The sky grumbled. It had turned a bruised color. Clouds formed a ceiling that threatened to collapse into pieces. Rain began, lightly at first. It thickened and fell hard onto my neck. The rain turned into hail. Hurrying out of the courtyard, like the others who had been strolling through, Zina stopped at a trolley, the Thirty-Seven. A young man in a ripped t-shirt and jeans and sporting a mullet took fares in the palm of his hand. He mumbled something difficult to understand. The trolley waited until the hail stopped. When it began to move, Zina had already sat down. The glass was cool.

At the other end of the car was a silent figure, none other than Jesus. It was impossible that He was anybody else. His hair was long and unkempt, wavy, with frizzy ends sticking up. His clothes were dirty. One arm, as if it had been impaled by a nine-inch stake, hung limp at His side. Odessan Jesus was ogling Zina, who had given her seat to an elderly woman. His lips twitched as if in prayer to Himself. Zina took my seat. Odessan Jesus shuddered. He attended Zina, until she warned Him without a sound. He sighed and moved to stand next to me. Smelling as if He had recently woken up on the surface of the Black Sea, He giggled to himself and squinted out the window. A spit bubble formed on His lip. One man, who was standing, said, *I'm thinking that I'll disembark.*

I'm thinking that too, said Odessan Jesus, a few words of apocrypha. The trolley lurched, and they hurried to force the doors open and exit. Before exiting, He stopped to blow a kiss to Zina, His Magdalene.

As the trolley started to move again, I switched arms. With my tired arm, I felt my back pocket, the pocket where my wallet should have been. It was no longer there. Odessan Jesus and His comrade had disappeared from the street. In English, I said to Zina, "The Flesh-Made-Word robbed me." That I had spoken English, nobody seemed to mind this time.

FOURTEEN
ZINAIDA OLEGOVNA

After the *zapoi*, Zina and Valinka disappeared from Odessa's streets for a whole day and into the next. She heard her papa enter, sigh, and leave, and then the sound of the door to the apartment being forced shut and locked. In English, she called out, "Valinka, you awake?" He groaned. She came to him, stood at the edge of his bed, and said, "I did that to make sure I still can. I haven't been with a man in a long time...You can tell about it if you want."

"I don't want," he said, sitting up. "I can keep silent."

"Good. Don't tell my papa. Catacombs are off limits for me."

Why? he asked her in Russian.

She searched for an answer and avoided his gaze. He really wanted to know, this boy. She mumbled, "A friend of my papa died there. Don't say a word to him about it."

When her papa returned, the man was quivering with rage. He put his bags on the kitchen table and crossed his arms. She didn't have to confess to him, and she merely stood, strutted past, and shut the door to her room. The wood of her door slid closed, the latch popped out again.

She heard Valinka trying to explain to her papa where they had been and what they had done without revealing anything. Instead of attacking Valinka, she knew well enough that her papa had knitted his brow before he sat down at the table. She heard him tap out the pattern on the tablecloth, and this tapping made her give a short hoot of laughter. He turned on the radio, cranked it. Anchors were discussing the many fights that had broken out in the *Rada*. The last one had been in January, when members of the *Svoboda* Party began to sling fists with one of the Communist Party members.

The window was open, and she turned her attention to the breeze, interrupted by Valinka stomping into his room. She opened her door, peeked out, and stepped into his. He was stuffing items into his backpack. He began to recite an Abramovich anecdote about Abramovich moving to America, being robbed, and trying to end with the English words, "The Americans beat the Russians."

"You made that one up, and it is shitty," Zina told him.

I, Valinka began in Russian, switched to English, "I'm keeping it secret, but he's kicking me out. Anyways, I knew it was gonna end one day. I love you, I guess. Anyways, *do svidaniya*. I guess you think I got all I wanted."

"Well, your anecdotes still suck," she said.

Valinka closed his eyes, hooted, and slapped his cheeks. When he had breathed a couple times, he opened his eyes, "Okay. Yes. *Do svidaniya*." His bag packed, he hefted it onto one shoulder and breezed past her.

Zina shrugged. "I can't talk to him. He betrayed me even worse than you. He kept it from me that my mama was in San Francisco." Valinka turned to stare at her. "Maybe I gonna leave too."

"Where you gonna go?"

"I don't know. You?"

"I don't know. Come with me?"

She shrugged. He shrugged and headed for the door. What a fine specimen she had made him. She rushed to her papa. *Papa, for both our sakes, help Valinka out. Volodya, your comrade.* Zina paused here. *He stole money from the poor American.* Another pause. *Maybe you'll retrieve it and everybody will be satisfied?*

Satisfied? her papa asked.

Valinka asked from the end of the hallway, *How much do I owe you?*

Her papa groaned, said, "Ah?"

"Will you come?" Valinka asked her.

"I can't leave him. Even though he betrayed me. That's...not what I can do."

Understood, Valinka said.

"Thank you. You don't sound American anymore." As she said this last sentence, he was leaving. Nonetheless, through the heavy, soundproof door she sent her voice.

She went back to not talking to her papa again. He hadn't understood the English, but he was silent nonetheless, not needing to appeal to her to stay. He knew she would. One morning, on her way out, she noticed that the clothes she had brought to him from the United States of America were hanging in the closet from a shelf support. That was where her papa left rags to dry. He had made rags of the expensive clothes from America.

She remembered how he had read the Tsvetaeva poem, *"Trying Jealousy,"* with the words, *How can you live with another woman?* and *You, who stood on Sinai?* He had meant it to be *another man*, to be about his woman living with another man. He didn't want to sacrifice the exact sound of it. If it were *How can you live with another man?* it would change the sound. Instead of the *zh* and the *shch* sounds in *woman*, there would be the *mu* and the *zh* sounds of *man*. It would take the sting of anger out of it. It was simply not a man's poem. So her papa had read it out loud as if he was already beyond Galya. Instead, it showed that he pined for that bitch. And Zina suspected him of finding satisfaction among the prostitutes who congregated on the Lanzheron Steps.

It was easy to switch to thinking about her new job at *Arkhiv Ekho* as well as her memories, unleashed like opening the *Drawer of Pandora* after the sex she'd had with Valinka. All of a sudden, she was remembering how a friend's papa who called that friend *Queen of Piss* and was nonetheless considered a good papa since he had stuck around, only to terrorize that friend's mama. And that friend's mama had nonetheless stuck around. Why had Zina's papa been forsaken?

She turned onto *Transfiguration Street* and remembered when, at seventeen, she had sniffed glue. Her papa had found out and stopped her before it had become too bad.

She turned on *Greek Street* to come back toward the Opera Theater, which she had passed further south, and remembered the recent movements and repetitions of her work at McDonald's. She remembered bussing tables at Ram's Horn. In almost every memory there had been something done wrong, a devastating misstep, like the one little demonstration she had attended, so minor, the one step that had ended her life in the United States of America. Now she could expect this devastating misstep to happen with *Arkhiv Ekho*.

But events that had been out of her control had also happened. Where had the misstep been when, back in Detroit, she had heard the knock at the screen door, the one that sounded like a dirty violin, a fiddle? Where had the misstep been when she heard a man's voice say, "Police," and she had said nothing and not moved? Where had the misstep been when the voice spoke Russian? *You home?* Zina had wished she spoke no Russian, did not understand the voice. She had not misstepped. She had done nothing for a long time until another voice said, "This is the police. Somebody from this home called us." She had waited longer. "Don't worry. We're not here for you. We're here for the Mexicans that live here." After some time had passed, the voice had said, "You dodged a bullet." The screen door had scraped as it shut, sounding like an Odessan fiddler. "*Do svidaniya*," the first voice had said.

Arkhiv Ekho was in Odessa's center, and as she entered the building, she inhaled its air, tried to anticipate the next devastating misstep. Like a good *Pioneeress*, she would be always ready.

It would probably have to do with her work, which was to translate computer files, TIFFs, which included the fingers, wrists, and forearms of the people who digitized the documents from which they were made. Where were those people now? They no longer worked at *Arkhiv Ekho*. Now she did.

These documents are located in safety in a climate-controlled space. People from all over the world can freely examine reproductions of them. It had been her job to translate these two sentences. In the first, she thought of the word for *safety*. It was literally *without danger*. It made her think that *danger*, shorter and easier to say, was the natural state in the Russian-speaking world. *Without danger* was climate control. It was unnatural.

Sitting there, staring at a computer screen, Zina considered that the problem was, once the text was in a computer, there was no need to look anymore. Paper was direct, not digital. Nonetheless, even digitized, the TIFF files of diaries and writings were not in English. They were not about Americans. And Americans were not fucking reading them. Zina's job was not simply to translate them. Dasha had made it sound as if it was also Zina's job to attract American readers, who would do research in and, ultimately, give money to the archive.

This part of the job was the real job. This part of the job was impossible, and it would lead to the devastating misstep in a hurry, she was sure. The computers exhaled hot air, generated by their panting over the TIFF files, which took up too much memory. The files did not only take up memory. They were difficult to read, much less translate. The handwriting was often tortured *chicken scratch*. They were also difficult to read because so many Ukrainians, so many Odessans, had said long ago and still said, *We don't do it that way*. They were difficult to read because the truth had been censored and suppressed. The truth itself was nothing more than that death was always alongside, that it was the white noise in the room, that it was the unsaid. It was impossible to attract American readers other than Valinka. She could put him on her resume. He was open. He listened.

But about other Americans, the majority, an Odessan voice growled into her ear, sneered really, letting each sentence end with a continuation of the last phoneme uttered. This sneer was similar to the Mancunian accent, only in Russian. Each sentence ended with a groan, perhaps a sigh, as if the speaker was sad to let her sound stop. *Ili.*

About the Odessan, maybe she did not know what she was talking about. Maybe, after all this time, she would have to admit that she had no idea. The truth this Odessan voice spoke was nonetheless real. They were difficult to read because these records of suffering were often very similar. In fact, they were often very much the same. And readers, especially Americans, would be bored. They needed it to be dressed up a little. What was the difference to them between Kolyma and Norilsk? They needed some sexy drama, a clear dime store conflict. Otherwise they yawned at torture that had caused voices—in a language they didn't know—to shriek. The translation made the voices in the language they didn't know almost impossible to distinguish. There is a difference between Aleksandr Solzhenitsyn, who hated Americans, and Varlam Shalamov, who might never have even met one. That had nothing to do with Odessa, Zina's American voice told her.

Once the devastating misstep had been taken, once this part of her life, like so many others, had come to an end, she would miss *Arkhiv Ekho.* All those texts, that building in the center of Odessa, it had been a ground for her, a place to land. She would miss hearing the steps of her coworkers throughout the building. Rebuilt after the Great Patriotic War, its floors had held for decades because they could bend. As she walked across those floors now, she thought of how she would miss the sounds of typing that made her long to sneeze from paper dust. The real archive was chattering from within cardboard boxes. The real archive was diaries, old and wrinkled and often misunderstood in the chattering. The Ukrainian government officially claimed that they respected the work. *Arkhiv Ekho* was in contact with the police, whoever they were.

A voice boomed in the first room of the office. A chair rolled and slammed to the floor. The boom said, *We wouldn't want this very important work to fall into the wrong hands, like those of the fascists in Kiev. So, we'll take some of these materials under our own protection.*

This voice caused her to fall back on her upbringing. Zina fell back into the hustle and drive, which an Odessitka inherits. Her arms, hands, and fingers began moving in concert to gather as much of the real archive, the paper and ink diaries themselves, as they could and place these items into her large bag. These items she treated like passports. She knew immediately with an unconscious genetic memory that she would need them to cross a border, or some other surface like that of the place where water meets air. On the other side, she was unsure whether she could breathe without these documents.

The voice sounded much like that of Volodya. The voice sounded like the version of his voice he used to disguise himself. It was a voice spoken from behind a mask.

Zina entered the room where Nastya and Dasha were trying to confront the men. *It's a matter of respect for the privacy of the witnesses and their families,* Dasha said. As another man started carrying a box out, she said, *Many of these are the only versions of such documents.*

More the reason, Volodya said.

Who are you? Under which authority do you act? Zina asked.

He turned his head to her and chuckled. He said, *We're Russians. We're Soviet, imperial patriots.*

Of what? Odessa? Is that a joke? God, she wished it was.

Who are you? Volodya asked. She waited for him to recognize her. Like a spear, or the horn of a shoulder plate to an elaborate, imperial suit of armor, something protruded from Volodya's torso and made his long coat hang awkwardly. Another man carried one of their boxes of documents out. Volodya spoke as if none of what was happening was happening, right next to him. *You know jokes? Anecdotes? Not bad.*

She was still riding under his memory's radar. *Why is there that line in the middle of the number seven? When Moses was telling the Ten*

Commandments, he came to the seventh, "Don't fornicate." A dude said, "Cross that one out!" Galya would be proud.

Jews, yes? Volodya mumbled.

Yes. Abramovich, nervous and shaking, comes to Transfiguration Cathedral. Everybody knows something's wrong, because from the beginning he crosses himself the wrong way, like a Catholic, or even worse. Abramovich asks to speak to the priest. "Batyushka," Abramovich says, "I was with a woman." The young priest nods. "Okay. Perhaps you should relax, young Christian. God forgives." Abramovich sighs. "You don't understand. I was with a second woman." The priest staggers. "I was with both women at the same time." The priest falls backwards, but he shakes it off, as if an invisible hand caught him. He becomes upright again. "This is something different. Were these women Christians?" Abramovich makes a sound that could be laughter, could be a sob. "How should I know? I'm a Jew. They certainly know that now." The priest's brow creases, forms the Roman numeral V. He chokes. "You're a Jew? Then, why'd you come here? Why are you confessing this to me?" Abramovich honks. "Is that a joke? I'm 'confessing' to everybody. I was with two women at the same time!"

Enough about Jews.

She was sure now that he would recognize her. He still stared as if his mask were a barrier to his awareness. Maybe a joke about Catholics would be better than one about Jews. *The Pope rides in a car in America. He says to his driver, "I'm the Pope. They never let me drive. I just want to drive once. Let me drive?" Later that day, at headquarters, one cop says to another, "Guess whom I stopped?" "Oh, okay. The mayor?" "Higher." "The governor?" "Higher." "Higher than the governor? You didn't pull over the president." "Higher than the president." "Nobody's higher than the president." "Look, I don't know who he was. But his driver was the Pope."* It was Zina's greatest moment, yet Galya was absent.

Good, Volodya said in his booming voice. *A pure Odessitka.* Meanwhile, the archivists-librarians watched with crucified eyes. Nastya gestured at the empty floor.

153

Please bring back those papers your comrade dragged out, Zina added as soon as the imagined applause had subsided.

I already said, it's for safekeeping. We won't reveal any of the names. He shuffled around the room, grumbling at every computer. Finally, he nodded at one, and the man who had been lifting boxes approached, unplugged the computer, and took it outside. *Why all this technology? Technology only betrays.*

Let's call the police. Larceny division. They can probably protect these items better than any of us.

Maybe. There are some good ones with the police. But there are also some with the Kiev junta.

Well, I'll tell them the jokes. Then, everything will be understood.

He watched her. *You could be my own granddaughter, girl.*

It took every ounce of will, every drop of blood, every strand of muscle in her body not to roll her eyes when he said that. Her smile could shatter glass, her nod could chop off a head. *This building is very sound.* He came close, and the scent of vodka brushed past like a blow from rotten flowers. *This building is very sound. We have direct contact with the Odessa police. If there is a security concern, we can call them to deal with it.*

Good. We're leaving. If you need some help, you know how to get in touch with us. He winked as if the mask would protect him.

My name is Zinaida Olegovna Bondarenko.

"*Ili,*" he said.

My father's Oleg Bondarenko.

Oh. The echo of this bounced within his skull for a few seconds. *A good man. But you're a lesbian kike. Who fucked one of our boys Anton in the catacombs.* His voice winked. *I know you.*

Volodya's stated knowledge broke in and echoed within her skull. It deafened her, as the man who had imparted it left the building.

Moments later, Dasha was dialing somebody on her cellphone as she stepped into the other room. Nastya remained, stunned, breathing like a fish out of water.

Zina burst out into laughter, and this hysterical laughter clearly disgusted Nastya. *Please, Zinaida Olegovna, calm down.* *I don't understand,* Dasha said. *There is no ideology here. There was information about the Soviets, but there was also information about Bandera. There was only evidence of crimes, committed by both sides.*

Zina left soon afterward. Everybody did, except for Dasha, who remained in the office, making call after call after call.

When she exited and was back in front of the building where *Arkhiv Ekho* was located, Zina began to remember, again, that night in Detroit. As she glided over the sunlit concrete, watching for the "Partisans"—they could be any of these people, exuding contentment without smiling, despite that their country was at war—she tried to remember every detail of the night that brought her back to these, her people. Of course, none of these Odessans had a weapon. Nobody was panting and grunting. Nobody was at the other's throat. They weren't smiling, but that's because all of them were suffering. Nobody was humming tunes or twiddling fingers. Yes, their suffering was all the same. Why should they kill one another? The only difference was what made each of them moan. For some it was an unsettled future, others an unsettled past. Better to have an unsettled future, of course, she thought. How do you like that logic? Volodya would call it Jewish logic, crooked, aching, like a pretzel. Their clothes were different now, synthetic, different shoes, less squeaky. These people defeated the Germans, didn't they? The faces were the same, even the ears twitched in the same way. The jokes sounded the same, maybe spoken a bit faster, maybe with more audible cursing. The sweet cut of the pleasures was still the same. They thought they were cowboys, tumbleweeds. But tumbleweeds, for these her people, tumbleweeds were losers, not heroes. Galya was a tumbleweed, a loner. Whatever she was, she was no longer an Odessitka. Zina stopped by a fiddler playing in front of the Lanzheron Stairs.

The fiddle was the key. That night that led to her leaving Detroit, leaving America and Galya, that night was forever evoked by the sound of that stupid screen door into Linda's basement apartment. It had sounded like an Odessan fiddler's scrape. That door she had opened after having opened the inside door. She closed the two doors, smirked at how stupid these doors were, stepped out, and stood in the stairwell leading down to their basement apartment. Above her was a small roof made of a strange rubber substance, which gave off a noxious smell that she could sense from underneath. She spit and listened for the splat, whether it would freeze and crackle. She stared at windows, licked by light from inside.

She knew the new year had come when gunshots clacked and boomeranged throughout the city.

"Zinaida Olegovich Bondarenko?"

"Olegovna," Zina said to the uniformed man who had appeared before her out of the noxious air.

"Whatever. I have some questions. You speak English?"

"Yeah," she said.

"Good. I got a guy here who speaks Russian if you gotta speak Russian."

"No."

"Were you arrested on November Eleventh, 2013?"

"Yeah."

"Will you come with me, please?"

As Zina began to climb the steps, the door flew open and she heard Valinka say, *Run, Zina!* In this country of itchy-trigger-finger cops, while it was dark and gunshots were going off in the surroundings, Valinka wanted to make a run for it. As the man in uniform put his hand on his hip and faced Valinka, she backed away and put her hands up. She said, "Hände hoch!" It was the only German she knew. Her papa, who had studied the Fascists' language, would be able to speak to these men. She backed up until somebody else took her arms down and handcuffed her. She had expected handcuffs. Like an Odessitka, she could laugh at this misfortune. She did so, out loud.

However, that somebody, who had taken her arms and hand-cuffed her, whispered in her ear, "*Ne nado*," a common enough Russian phrase, appropriate to the situation. If Linda had heard, she would have thought that last word, *nado*, with its unaccented *o* that sounded like an *a*, was the Spanish word nada, nothing. No nothing? No nothing means something. That somebody left Zina standing there facing the wall with that phrase "*ne nado*" echoing in her mind. The echoing phrase replaced her breathing. She began to hyperventilate. She could hear the first cop ordering Valinka to his knees and how Valinka, *thank God*, was obeying. As they must have been putting handcuffs on him, Valinka yelled, *Leave her. She didn't do anything!* and "If we were POCs, you would have killed us!" It sounded so cheesy that she chuckled, and with this bit of laughter she forced herself to slow her breathing, to stay conscious.

When she came home from *Arkhiv Ekho*, came home from the raid on it, she asked her papa if there was such a thing as Odessan patriots today.

His answer was, *Is that a joke?*

FIFTEEN

OLEG

When her boyfriend walked out the door, Zina said to Oleg, *Help him, papa. I love him.* He stayed seated. *Good,* she said, *That's not it. But he's one of us,* she said. He stayed seated. *Okay, maybe he's not one of us. But it will be bad if an American goes to ruin on our streets, especially these days.* At these words Oleg stood and moved into action. And his daughter was pleased.

But the boyfriend was already out the door, into the elevator, and off.

Later, Zina commanded, *You go and get that money from Volodya. Also, he took some things from where I work.*

Oleg stopped. *I understand, Zina. It's not about your friend alone. You want something else from Volodya.* It would please her. She would love him again. *I'm your spy,* he said to his daughter. This verbal wink was all that needed saying between these two psychics.

Volodya and his ramshackle house required preparation. Oleg left his money and dressed in stained clothing. Before departing, he sat down at the kitchen table to prepare himself, saying to Zina, *If he asks about me, I'll say everything's in order. If he asks about women, I'll say I'm a bachelor and want to stay that way.* Zina rolled her eyes at that one. *Seriously. I'm tired of women.*

Zina told him that his old comrade from the *Flot* had joined the separatist movement, *Odessa Partisans.*

Oleg rode his bicycle. The air was empty, quiet, and cool, humming with potential activity. He was used to such mornings because of his swims. He passed the rusty body of the old Zhiguli, the spray-painted word *TUPIK*. Volodya had always denied any connection with the stripped car.

Why do you help him if he's such an asshole, papa? Zina once asked. Oleg answered, *He's old. He was a good neighbor in the nineties. That is, in the difficult times.*

The next signpost was a rusty drill bit, half the length of his body and a whole decimeter in diameter. The drill bit was embedded on a forty-five-degree angle at the gap in the corrugated metal fence bordering Volodya's property. It looked ready to impale a clumsy person or child. Volodya called such traps his *technology*.

Oleg wheeled his bicycle through the maze right up to the step where Volodya stood. The old man pointed his chin at the sky. His hand rested on his hip as if on the butt of a pistol. Oleg gently rested his bike against one of the pieces of *technology*. He was relieved that he had not triggered anything. *My friend, time tears from me every day. Tears and tears*, Volodya said. His chin moved along the air in the same trajectory as a violin's bow. *Doesn't it seem that way to you, comrade?*

Well, yes. That's why I come to you. To pick up the pieces. Volodya chuckled. However, whatever had loosened coiled back up. Oleg lifted a faded tarp and glanced underneath.

Volodya barked, *Leave it.* Oleg frowned and dropped the canvas. Volodya was gathering breath to give a speech about the wrecks in his yard. *Actually, take off the cover. That's what you'll help me with. It's a generator. I want to fix it, and increase the electricity in the house.* While Volodya was speaking, Oleg looked the generator over. It was in better condition than most of the objects lying around Volodya's yard. The frame had succumbed to rust, though other metallic segments were still clean. Oleg searched with his hands for a way to wire the generator. *Well, first off, it needs to work. Then we'll hook it up to the house. That's another problem. I don't know if I can fix it, Volodya. This technology's older than me.*

I'll help. It's not older than me. I can orient you around it. I just can't see the small parts. And I need your hands.

Understood, Volodya. But, may I ask, why do you want more electricity in your house? What's there that's drinking up all the electricity?

The old man flinched. His arms folded like iron. Oleg stared beyond him at the dark, mute door. The only machine he could think of that took much electricity was a refrigerator. There was an air conditioning unit in the bedroom, though he could not imagine Volodya ever using A. C. *Maybe, Volodya, I can help you with the refrigerator. Is it not working so well? Maybe it's too old. C'mon, show it to me.*

Volodya surveyed his *technology* as if to praise it. *It's not the refrigerator. I just want more electricity.* Oleg kicked the machine. Volodya blurted, *Look. I need to be on the computer. Some boys will come to help me out. But I need more electricity.*

Who are these boys?

The Odessan Partisans. Fighting for our rights in Novorossiya. We're planning a demonstration in Kulikovo Field, outside the Trade Union Building, Second of May.

What would Volodya blurt if he knew that Oleg thought anybody who used the name *Novorossiya* had succumbed to pro-Putin propaganda? *Understood,* Oleg said. Odessans did not abide No Secrets Between Sailors. Oleg said, *I won't mess. I'll help.*

Volodya's breathing caught in his throat. Soon enough, Oleg would not have to worry about him. Volodya sat on the steps, creaking the way sodden wood does. In the distance, a wrecker was smashing a Soviet building. Volodya would be there at night to salvage pieces of material left behind.

Remember that metal detector we fixed? You still go out on the beach and find things? Oleg asked.

Volodya laughed. "*Da,*" he said, his face positioned within a beam of sunlight. *Like we used to do with your little girl. I can give you a little compensation.*

No. It's one of her boys. He was at the beach a couple days ago. I think you took some money from him. Volodya wheezed. Oleg concentrated on the generator. *Maybe you could give back his money?*

I'll give his money to you, friend. I wouldn't steal from you or your family. Where's he from?

American.

Fucking Americans. Take so many of us to their fucking palaces. But they're palaces built on sand, you know? They come for me? It won't be pretty, even if they win. I'll make the fight bad for them. I'll make it cost a lot of their money.

Thank you, Volodya, Oleg answered. He took what sounded like his first breath in Volodya's yard. His fingers had tripped over the same articulation inside the generator several times. *Volodya,* he started, *tell how it was. You remember? How it was in the time of "Khryak?" Isn't that what people called Khrushchev?* He knew how to win over older folks by using nicknames like *Khryak* for Khrushchev.

Volodya gurgled. Oleg noted that he had never seen the man eat. The gurgle took on a rounder sound, more like laughter. Nostalgia radiated from the generator's parts, similar to those inside the submarine during their days in the *Flot.* Volodya's hand knocked against his shoulder. *There, friend. There's your money.* The hand held three hundred *hryven.*

That was all that Valya had lost, why Oleg had gone there, risked his life in some ways. Why would an American become so upset over so little? Like he understood the value of even a small amount of money, the difference it can make, the bargaining power of it, the fine lines between various gradations of poverty?

Anyways, he had not gone there for the American and his money. He had gone there because Zina had asked. He would do anything for her.

But he knew the day would come that Volodya would turn on him. *Democracy came too soon to us here, comrade,* Volodya had always said about the end of Soviet rule. Oleg swallowed what he had said the other day about how democracy had come. He had ended it there. It did not need saying. *I can tell you one thing about that time, the time of Khryak,* Volodya laughed. *I can say, that, back then, people helped one another. Simple people, like us, not apparatchiks,*

not bureaucrats. Simply the people. We looked after each other then. Even your generation understood that. But now, the youth don't understand. Like your daughter. Does she understand? What's she doing now?
   She works for a library near the City Center. The Echo Archive.
   Volodya gurgled for a long time. It lasted for almost a minute as if a snake were reversing out of his bowels and throat.
   Oleg knelt again and hugged the dusty body of the generator. It could work. Say what his daughter would about politics, the news, he would set all of that aside for working with Volodya on a spring afternoon, junipers blooming, a breeze lifting the dirt off the yard and sounding within the rusty shapes and traps as if they were within a Soviet realist portrait of simple, hard work. It was better than green paper and democracy. He crabbed to the side to approach the generator. It would be like his days in the *Flot*, out on the open sea. The old captain at his shoulder, heels clicking against steel, uniforms of garish colors, especially red, that had not yet faded with time.
   He's a real Russian man. Those like him aren't around anymore, he said to Zina that day, when he had returned.

SIXTEEN

ZINA

After her papa returned and idealized his time with Volodya, Zina stopped her reading for a moment to say, *Papa, even sailors' daughters know that sailors rarely see the light of day, much less the open sea. Not everybody gets to serve atop.*

She had been looking at the documents she had managed to rescue, saying to herself, *Mama left me. Papa kept me. But, from these texts, I will try to resuscitate a body of witness.* The wry, deadly humorous voice of Galya responded to this CPR metaphor with, Your CPR training expired, honey. You didn't save nobody.

Among the documents was the journal entry of an Italian *polit-emigrant* named Sapienza — only his last name was left. While sipping tea with others in the *House of Polit-Emigrants*, he had brought up Germany. In Germany they had begun arresting Communists, Sapienza wrote. Everybody agreed, especially the Germans in the group, that they were lucky to be in the Soviet Union.

Another *polit-emigrant* mentioned how the United States of America only recognized the Soviet Union at that time, not long before the *Great Patriotic War.* Ideas such as, "Imperialism is the final phase of Capitalism," were passed around this table where sat these foreigners in the Soviet Union. Sapienza ensured the group that they were on the right side of history.

The most interesting story, in the end, was how the diary of such a patriot ended up in the hands of *Arkhiv Ekho.*

In 1937, Sapienza wrote about how interesting it was that soldiers had begun to wear epaulets. At first he thought they would be kinder. In the library to which he and the other *polit-emigrants* had access, he found a book which depicted the tsar's guards, also wearing epaulets. This coincidence gave the ex-patriot pause. It might have been why his diary ended up where it did. His fate was unknown.

In another, a young man described his arrest. The man told of how a black Volga stopped in front of his apartment in the early evening. An Odessan, the young man said, *I know how to go by foot*, he said to the men inside the Volga. Also Odessans, they insisted that they spare his poor legs and kindly drive him to the office where an appointment had recently been made for him. The young Odessan man was a translator from English into Russian. When she read this, Zina saw herself as that young man in that NKVD office. Zina sits in the stiff and whiny chair, reminding her of her fifth class teacher, Anastasia Rostislavovna Sadnikova. Zina is the translator from English into Russian. The man interviewing Zina asks why he changed a word from *serious* to *difficult*. The man said, *Your comrade Nikolai Anatolevich wrote that the jobs of American workers are* "serious." *Why did you correct Nikolai Anatolevich in such a way?* The translator Zina tells him that he translated what was written, that the word "difficult" better carried over the specific meaning of what he said. The interviewer says, *You understand that here, in our country, in our great country, we don't complain about work. You understand this? We must have strength. It's important to our place in society. If a worker's weak, he shouldn't be a citizen. If he's weak, he's not a comrade, not a man, immoral.*

They let the translator go. He believed it was all because he had identified the documents which he was translating as technical instructions from Ford Motor Company in Detroit, Michigan. They were stolen, and he had foolishly mentioned his discovery to his supervisor. The journal ended after this entry.

Her favorite was a woman named Sonya Katko who needed to travel to Pavlinka to see her second cousin, who had given birth to a baby boy. She set out on foot. At more than twenty kilometers, it was a day's journey. A motorcyclist stopped along the road and offered to take her. She sat behind him, hugging his torso. He began to grope her body with his left hand. He only steered with one hand, and she mentioned in a joking manner that he would kill both of them. He said not to worry, that he had done this one hundred times. She jumped off, landed hard on her knees, and rolled into a field of canola. The motorcyclist continued on his way. He did not stop to complete his hundred and first time. Both her knees bloody, she limped the rest of the way. When she arrived, it was explained to her that her knee cap was separated. No matter. She was overjoyed to find the baby alive. She laughed and cried along with the baby, stayed by him through the night.

He was not her child, yet he brought her a joy that dulled pain.

Zina saw the word *kolgosp*, the Ukrainian version of *kolkhoz*. In a later entry, Sonechka wrote in ink deeply embedded into the page:

Here's a tale of four brothers and one sister. The kolgosp turned to buzzing rot in the fields. Our tractors no longer chuckled. Citizens argued through teeth, were forced to punish one another. Across the steppe the wheeze of hatred. I was able to study and scribble the record for the kolgosp. First, it was the beet crop, smaller and less than we expected. When my brother Stas refused to work the day after we sold the crop for kopecks, they arrested him. My mama's veins began to show. The onions did poorer than expected. They arrested Vitya for demanding a higher price for the few onions. Mama's hair turned white. Seryozha, in a meeting, demanded the utmost punishment, his voice broad and resonant. He said if what his brothers did was so bad, it should be known across the entire Soviet Union. When they arrested him, mama's throat went dry. Since I was educated, I recorded. After word spread about the poor yield of the kolgosp, the people's commissar accused me of theft, that I snuck our goods out somewhere, gave them to capitalists, for a profit that nobody could locate. But they took it easy on me, a poor woman, with my last, invalid brother, Gleb. We're here now in Odessa. I just want to be an Odessitka. I won't say a thing to anybody.

Later, this Sonechka wrote:

I'm in the Odessa Prison of Special Purpose No. 1. On Big Fountain Avenue. My mother said, "Words drip from your mind like dew from acacias." She said, "You must write this all down, in order to prove to the sovet what they have done to us." I wrote it down, mama. Nobody read it. Nobody saved you or anybody in our family. Writing, recording, knowledge bring trouble to people. Truth should be a violent woman, victor over illusion. There's no need for her to demonstrate her strength. She hobbles lies, makes them legless. She's dangerous. Now all I have is this thick stem of a bottlebrush to clean my teeth. The ink's a little blood. I hide the pages. I unstitched the binding, rolled them inside a rubber sheath, which I insert underneath and inside myself.

The guard asks me, "So, you are against all war?" I say, "You're for all war?" The guard laughs. "Of course not. But, if there's no other choice, if war's the only possibility," she says. She sucks her upper lip against her teeth. I say, "If there's no other choice, I choose no war." She says, "What? You made a mistake in Russian. I had in mind, that there would be no other choice but war." I reply, "No choice but war's even less probable than no choice but peace. War's complicated. What's more natural, war or peace?" She nods, says, "Natural." I say, "If you can't talk about all war, why talk about all peace? Or, if you can't talk about all peace, why talk about all war? Everything's complicated." She says, "So, you agree there are times war may be necessary?" I answer, "No. I disagree. But I won't say anything about everything. Only, like a child, I think that peace is simpler. When it's complicated, somebody's making it that way." She asks, "Can a person defend his land, at least?" I say, "Yes, he can. She can too. But they send us Ukrainians away to defend Finland."

I'd die defending the land between Kiev and Odessa. She's fruitful, despite the mistakes of the kolgosp. Beets and potatoes grow almost everywhere. Nobody harvested them. The soil gives, no matter what happens on its surface.

I'll tell how they made the new road to Tairovsky Cemetery. Work begins with one man, who clears and widens the road with a staff in this shape |. The guards won't give them a scythe unless absolutely necessary. In the morning they cut back any flora surrounding the road with a tool shaped like this У. All must be seen and heard and wide enough for trucks. There are those who widen the flanks of the road, then those who flatten the road out. One man digs ditches. He receives a shovel. Another man who receives a shovel chops up the crest between the ruts using three cuts in this shape И. The one who follows behind him pats the chopped road down with his bare feet. He is the last, like the letter Я. The men sing while they work. Once they're done, they repeat the song. It becomes a meditation in this way, a holy chorus. If they ever reach a kilometer, they toe its edge. If they have time, they lay the stones they've broken along the sides of the road. Some stones are large enough that the guards give them a sledgehammer to break them. It often takes care of bumps to sledgehammer a stone against them. Although this is the loudest sound they've ever heard, it is quiet and still out there across the steppe. Sometimes they make new holes, and they have to dig out the moist soil and mix it with the top layer of dust, which might blow away, flattened out across the expanse. All the same, that's the end. They can do it with or without scythes, shovels, and sledgehammers. The way without is quieter but takes longer.

They advise, asked to or not. The guards say, "You're not slaves. You're worker-citizens in the Socialist Utopia. You must work. Work is a matter of honor, glory, valor, and heroism. Without work, a person's simply a social parasite." One, a man named Vyron, says, "You work for the people since you robbed the people, if you didn't work. To justify yourself, you must work. And work is *a matter of honor, glory, valor, and heroism. In the judgment of the people, it will be counted."*

Maybe they'll send me to Magadan. I'll definitely speak slowly. If a person speaks with speed, it means the person is afraid. The person's probably from a higher class than many, even though some of these are an exception and speak slowly and with deliberation. Fast talkers are often less interested in listening than others, and they're almost always sure of whatever it is they said, so sure that they would never let a person ask questions about that.

If only we could all lie down and nestle one another. Instead God treats us all as if we were blatniye.

This last word Zina recognized as the descriptor for criminals, specifically Soviet criminals. There were songs, slang, and many many tattoos associated with such words.

I think we failed to do something. There's something we didn't recognize, a path we didn't take. In this society, truth is a matter of life and death. If somebody's truth and that of the sovet don't align, that somebody works, then he dies. Not like in the United States of America, where truth is not as important as that the product continues to sell, that business continues along a smooth and graded road. This is the difference between reality and capitalism. Truth is hard on us, though.

It's hard even just to tell a story. You want to leave things out, forget. The brain wants to forget, I say. It wants to forget what we did. We want to. We aren't better, even if we love a citizeness — I always call women citizenesses — We aren't better because we kill those who don't work.

We can't even see the sun rise and fall. There's the rancid smell of the wadding on which we sleep, spots of wetness where we drool. The flight of the canvas above is like smooth skin, curved out. Flies bite at our bare legs. When it becomes hot in the middle of the day, we often wish to remove more clothing. Heat makes everything

*heavy, but it's not as burdensome as frost. During winter the body
loses touch with itself and becomes ice.*

Like memories, Zina needed to let these stories take over. Their
sounds were more important than others. They gave her solace,
and she read over them out loud like a child murmuring herself
to sleep.

A memory of Galya kept returning to her. An atheist, Galya
once quoted the First Letter to the Corinthians, Chapter Thirteen:
Love...protects all, trusts all, has hope in everything, bears all. Zina only
knew it was the Bible because Galya told her. What did Galya bear?
She read a poem by Afanasy Fet. A tear burst out of the dark wood
of her eyes and sprinted downhill along her cheek. Now it was all
coming back to Zina. Galya had begun to tell her about working
with a woman who had lived through the occupation of Odessa.
The woman told Galya about how, during mobilization, she had
wanted to walk along the beach. The beaches were forbidden.
When the Fascists dropped bombs on Odessa before the ground
invasion, it was no longer forbidden. One bomb hit a cruiser,
transporting people out of the city. Small boats, the ones used for
fishing, were sent out to rescue those who had fallen into the sea.
Once those people were on board, the small boats transported the
people back to the shore. They were delivered to the *Archaeological
Museum*, where a makeshift hospital had been set up, where the
woman worked. One of those rescued from the sea was a woman
Galya's coworker promised never to name. The secrecy of it reminded Zina of what she had read at the archive. It also brought
back another memory.

At the time Zina had known that she should listen to her
mama. Too bad she only half-listened. The story was lost. Now it
returned.

The woman never needed a name. Zina decided to call her Sonya. Sonya cried for Galya's acquaintance to be there with her.
The woman came and dusted the bread of Sonya's hand. Sonya

was simply a girl from the Ukrainian countryside. The woman, an Odessitka, could hear it in her voice. The woman kissed the air around her, sang folk songs to her, caught her body tossing itself on the bed, gave her the chalk dust they used as a placebo for medicine — they had no medicine, but could they say this? No. — For three days this happened.

One of the other nurses whispered in the woman's ear that they would lose Sonya to either her wounds or the summer cold that had come over her. The woman began to pray for Sonya. It was the first time the woman, a typical Odessan atheist, ever prayed. *Lord, the One God, whose Son is Jesus Christ, bring this woman back into our world, dirty and unhappy as it is, even if she didn't want this life.*

Afterward, Sonya told her, *That's the only time "Request and to you will be given" worked.* Sonya said, *Take it back.* With her finger, Sonya accused her own smiling face. *Put that pillow right here and hold it.* After three more days, Sonya gave up on death. Having given up on death, Sonya told her story.

I am a girl from the country. All I can say is that it is between here and Kiev. I went to school. I learned how to count. I could count how all of my brothers were disappearing. Nobody but me was left to count. The kolgosp had a low yield. They accused me of undercounting. They accused me of theft of money. None of it was true, but they had to hide the low yield, you understand? It would have made others in the oblast council fall into trouble as well. Don't mention this to anybody. I only tell you because soon I won't be here. Freedom that's called.

The women usually went to Odessa to sell products. I did too. My new job, punishment, was to clean the political emigrants' center. Don't look that up.

Sonya recited the same poem by Afanasy Fet in order to calm herself. Some days later, Sonya disappeared.

While the Occupation continued, the woman with whom Galya worked had become a maid for a high-ranking officer in the government of Transnistria. His wife appeared only to want to eat pickled herring for the rest of her life.

That was the end of the story of the woman Galya met. She had ended up working alongside Galya. Her story had affected Galya so much that it had caused Zina's mama to cry, to recite the Bible and poetry. It was the only time, Zina realized, that her mama had ever cried in front of her. Galya said, *I was there when she was dying. I held my hands over her body. I don't know why. I thought maybe I could draw out the cancer, beat the shit out of it. She said to me, "Galinka, now I'll relax. I'll relax. But listen. The woman I didn't want to name,"* the woman Zina had given the name Sonya, *"that woman is I! I am Sonya!"* After Sonya finished telling her story, Galya sat there in silence. Outside, they could hear the wind.

Zina, home alone, could hear the wind too. She even thought she could hear the violence in Kiev. Now she had found Sonya's words. She wanted to sit down and write to Galya. *Mama, was her name Sonya? I found her diary, mama!*

Instead she opened a small box she had managed to save, Sonya's items. There was a rucksack made of burlap, tied with a piece of string, two swaths of cloth, the softer swath the deepest inner layer, a piece of wool. There was a piece of silk with some hairs on it. Whose hairs? Zina felt that this question was more important than anything she had ever wanted to know. There was a soapstone for sharpening a knife. There was no knife. There was a piece of striped cloth, like one of her papa's shirts from the *Flot*.

Galya once sang *"The sun comes up and goes down,"* which Zina had found out was from a *blatnoi*, a criminal, song. It was the kind of song crooned to pass time in a prison cell. She said Sonya sang that.

Zina heard the birds and listened to them. She even laughed. Odessan birds joked.

She returned to the version of Sonya's journal she had:

171

*German. To me it's noise. Ukrainians say, They work hard. Every-
thing is "tsur ordnunk." And they bathe themselves regularly. They
have the most humane army in the world. They're coming to bring
German humanism to our wild Asiatic land. Abramovich says,
Tolik Guberman returned from Germany, and he said "German
humanism" means to beat kikes on the mug. The guard says, "Our
boys will take them down. No need to fear." I say, "If I must eat one
more spoonful of balanda..."*

Zina had to look it up. *Balanda* was trash soup. It was something horrible with a beautiful name.

Sonya:

*But I must eat balanda, no matter how much I want to choke,
mutely, into silence.*

*The guard talks me up. "We know you won't want to escape. In
the end of ends, they didn't send you to Siberia, or Magadan. Here
in the Ukraine, you have your food." She gestured at my bowl. "The
Germans will put you to work too, only worse. They'll treat you like
animals. Fascists have absolutely no respect for human life. They
imprison people and kill them. That is the very definition of what
a fascist is." I write her words. Maybe they will help me. They won't
help me.*

*These adjectives and nouns. "Whisper, shy breath/ The trill
of a sparrow/ Silver and flickering/ Of a dreamy stream// Light
nightly, nightly shadows/ Shadows without end/ A line of magical
changes/ To a dear face// In smoky puffs purple pink/ The shimmer
of amber/ And a kiss and tears/ And sunrise, and sunrise."*

It was the very same poem. There were no verbs. Of course,
many people knew and recited poetry regularly.

*Doom was his path. Since he has the same name as the great Rus-
sian poet, I made him learn by heart. "I loved you — perhaps love has*

still/ not altogether died in my soul/ but let it bother you no longer/
I do not want to sadden you at all// I loved you without-words, with-
out-hope,/ with shyness, with jealousy, tormented/ I loved you so sin-
cerely, so tenderly,/ as God would grant you to be loved by another."

Magic was happening. Zina told it to hush. She repeated Pushkin's word *bezmolvno*, a strange old word for *without words* or *no
words*.

Sonya:

*My hand is callous. Shattered skin scratches the still soft part of the
skin of my thigh, close to where it meets the torso. I don't blame.
Not the Ukrainians or Russians or Romanians or even Germans.
Nobody. But my wounds cry revenge. These openings will never
heal shut. I have not done enough. I need some witticism to say
here. But I just go quiet. Even blame is just words.*

*Words like raindrops. Word. Word. Word. I sleep soundly un-
der the rain. Like last night, until when I heard the shout, "Run!"
A voice said, "They'll kill you tomorrow." Then only thunder and
heavy rainfall, what sounded like the laughter of distant machine
gun fire. Is the world outside in a seizure of laughter? I could see, in
the hallway, two people lying on the floor. They appeared stamped,
deflated, flattened by lifelessness. "They fell. The roof collapsed on
them," said a man guard. But the roof was still above, of course.
There was a low growl, like a distant tractor. It was a guard himself
who made noise. "I cut their throats," he said. The bodies were only
real, not a true loss. Only real, not true.*

*Believe these words or not, this happened. The man guard came
to my cell and gave me a cigarette. I asked for the candle to light
it. "Where are you from again? Ah, Uman. You're no Odessitka
then. An Odessitka would know, if you light on a candle, you'll kill
a sailor." When I didn't say thank you, he said, "You think niggers
in Africa have it so good, comrade? When the Germans come, you'll
simply say, "ofene shtat," open city. And niggers in Africa don't even*

have to worry about the cold," he said. His hands scraped across the table. Outside a boneshaker wagon passed. He wouldn't look at me. His words made a ricochet against the wall. But this man, hissing murderer, and I share the same words, understood better than blood. When I finished the cigarette, he unlocked the cell. He said, wordlessly, to follow. The others were gathered in a large room. A whole room of people without sound. Just a rumbling outside. He cleared his throat several times, pushed out air. This piston sound was never audible. It was before dawn. If nobody were awake, our steps would slither and slip away on the dust. But people watched in silence. Then the whole world became the crash of a bomb, another kind of absolute filled our ears. It urged us toward the shore, into a boat. "Are you going to bury us?" I asked, not expecting an answer. "At sea," he answered not expecting that he would. Then the bombs came in lined patterns, regular, like they were magnets, whose force slammed them up against the world.

Well, we were in the water by then. One woman was pregnant. He heaved up, didn't speak, then vomited on the water. But nobody said stop. Nobody tried to help him. He saw himself in the water, troubled as it was, and maybe he would have told us he didn't want to follow his orders to kill us. But a wall of water rose up and split the boat. I fell in, held on to the bow.

I'm half fish, it seems. I should be dead already. I heard the great music that comes and takes each of us away. But then a small boat came. I fell to its deck, died, and gasped back to life in a bed, in a small house in Peresyp. My first question, Are these words still within me? Yes. Yes. Once again, yes. What am I more than these words now? The deepest black noise slid into my ear and then back out. Why can I still speak language and others can still understand me? These words didn't help conceal me at all. I only concealed them. My rescuers told me, "Earlier, you could go in to the catacombs through the Archaeological Museum. But they closed this entrance. Now you must go south, join with the women walking into town. You know them? I hear there's an entrance in Tairovsky

Cemetery. It's called "hedgehoggies." Don't write that down. Avoid Odessitkas.

Once she finished with Sonya's, Zina decided to read a diary entry written by a woman named Zinaida Olegovna Bondarenko during the first week of 2014 in a place called Detroit:

They arrested me. The man who arrested me said, "Ne nado."
I thought, perhaps, Anton traveled here, told our secret to this Russian-speaker and returned home. How else could he know what those words mean to me? How could somebody from ICE know? It was probably embarrassing for them. First they mistakenly didn't deport me even though I was a dangerous foreign woman. Now they arrested Valinka too since he was speaking Russian when they arrested me. They discovered soon after that he was a citizen, sooner than the time of the protest, when they didn't discover that I wasn't one. Yet he remains by my side like a dog. He talked today about Henry Ford, about how he walked along the catwalk above and stared down at the workers. At lunch time, the workers had to sit on the floor right in their places. Ford walked the catwalk, watched them, like an animal of prey.

When I asked him how he knew about things that happened decades before his birth, he shrugged. Also in the courtroom was a family speaking French. The father said, "Je m'en fou," which I heard some time before. I couldn't remember what it means, but I started to repeat it after that.

Valinka talked over me. He quoted a couplet that rhymed in Russian, For the right word, pity neither your mother nor your father.

Don't pity papa? Of course I don't pity him. When I come home, it will end his loneliness. Like he in Odessa, I walked along Michigan Avenue and counted out loud the leaves on the elm trees. Papa counts in Odessa, very fast. I can hear his quick counting, the numbers all slurred together. I can smell the "pryanyi" smell. I asked Valinka what "pryanyi" is in English.

"Pryanyi?" he repeated. "I don't know that word." He asked me about a book called, "Red Diaper Babies." I shook my head. When that didn't work, I placed my face in my palms. He waited for my answer. All around us were families. Children. Crying babies. None of them had red diapers. One baby shrieked, and a law enforcement officer nearby turned. I watched him. What the officer's face said about his thoughts was that this child was not a child. It was an animal that was in the wrong place, and the officer was a humble herdsman. "Je m'en fou," I said. A man cried. A man. Maybe Galya's lover cried, and she pitied him. But Galya wouldn't like that. I listened for how Valinka would cry for me. If papa saw an American cry for me, it would be the sweetest revenge. He cried for Galya. Why shouldn't an American cry for his daughter?

The court here is more orderly than it would be in Odessa. Not that I know. But I walked by the building there, home. I saw the Odessan lawyers, dressed like pimp hipsters.

I said to Valinka, "I never got to see Michigan Central Station."

He shrugged, said, "Not bad. Similar to 'Grand Central Station.'"

"I never got to see New York," I said.

He said, "Nothing grows there. Products arrive by truck and leave by garbage boat. Capitalists march back and forth. They eat those real goods. Their capital grows. If the island were to sink into the sea, it would only affect the amount of capital in the USA. The proletariat who worked there in sweatshops moved to Detroit. Henry Ford paid better. But he demanded his workers be automata. There was no ownership of the means of production under his model. The revolution in this country should have come in the industrial parks of Detroit. Detroit's the only salvation for the USA." When I looked at him, he said, "What? I'm nervous."

They let me use the toilet. It had small black tiles that glinted. An American voice said, "Don't cry."

When I returned to the courtroom, I noticed the flags. The flags were mute. Flags are only good if they flap in the wind. That is the only way a flag can mean something. It's even better if the flag is ripped, barely distinguishable, a rag as much as a flag. The American flag has the same colors as the Russian. But the Michigan state flag has similar colors to the Ukrainian. A small boy who wrestled in his mama's arms repeated, "Fag. Fag. Fag." He pointed at the flag next to the bench where the judge sat.

Valinka went to his knees, bowed his head, lifted it slowly, reached for my hand, took it, and said, "Can I be your husband?" He was confused. He glared at me out of his confusion. He didn't know how to propose in Russian.

"Fag. Fag. Fag!" said the little boy.

"I can't marry you," I said. "I'm a fag." As expected, Valinka gasped at the pejorative. He sat back, stared at his hands in his lap. An American needs to feel hopelessness. It's so scarce here. Hopelessness here is like hope itself in Ukraine. In Odessa, Valinka would be as baffled as I am here.

A lawyer working for the state explained to me that I could voluntarily depart from the country. If I bought my own ticket, I could leave without further detention. They would deport me later on. And, if I stayed, I'd have to marry Valinka. He called it "voluntary return." It was time to make a decision that would change my life. Papa talked about the only time Boris Grebenshchikov came to Odessa. At the same time, there was an earthquake in Odessa. Coincidence? Should I have answered Valinka's proposal with another? To ride with me to Ukraine? Would he understand my Grebenshchikov example? It's not mine. It's Papa's. Would he understand "earthquake"? Shaking? Everything is happening so fast. He proposed wrongly. I refused, sort of. Life is always so. But now I feel everything. The past and the future, all bombards me while I sit and idle, hands in my lap.

Behind the bench something wound up. Again, I asked to use the toilet. I was told I didn't need to ask. There I coughed, and it echoed *across the space. The wind outside howled through a vent. I waited. I waited for one of the mouths to tell me what to do. I waited for it to say to me,* "Listen. This is happening to you. Do not try to understand. You never will. And would it help, if you understood? No fucking way. People love to name things. But what is this? It happens to you, and it will take you out of this country. It don't matter how smart and beautiful you are. You can be a special princess. It don't matter. It is kicking your ass out. But the end has not yet come. You are better than this place. But you must run, girl. Run. Your papa will send you money. And take that crazy American with you.

This little voice in a sea of black puckered mouths said to me, "Tough titties about your mama. But you must move. Look at you. They expect you...look at you! They expect you to recognize their institutions, their culture? You?" *It simply came out. I knew that I must take this deal. I'm doing the* "voluntary return." *I'm going home. It feels good to have control over such a significant action. There's so little in life that we can say we control.*

Her mama could have been Sonya or any Odessitka or Ukrainka. Her mama could be simply Ukraina. She could lay her body across Odessa's lap and let the sarcastic tones, the wave of the Black Sea, the grass and sea smell, overcome her. She could fall asleep in Odessa's arms, the Lanzheron and the Potemkin Stairs each, rigid, worn, still sturdy, still holding.

SEVENTEEN
OLEG

O leg had almost been with an *Amerikanka* once a long time ago, so long he almost forgot. She had come to Odessa to take care of family business. She was born in Odessa, but she had left at so young an age that she barely spoke the language. Yet there was business to take care of, and she, an *Amerikanka*, could take care of business. Her family had owned some seaside property, and there were some items which a friend of a friend had asked Oleg to take care of.

From the moment he met her, he could tell that Sandra wasn't an Odessitka. She didn't have the fried vocals of one, the kind of voice that carries the sigh and rasp of the Old World. Also, she didn't know Russian. She knew *da, nyet*. Everybody knows that. The word to go home was important: *domoi*, emphasis on *moi*. It ended up that the property they were taking care of was unable to be her home. She had to live with Oleg. What about the word for hungry, *golodnaya*, Oleg asked. She didn't want to eat? Some Odessitkas are stubborn and go all morning without food.

From Zina's boyfriend, Oleg had learned that nobody wants to be who he really is. He remembered that Sandra also didn't want to be American. All the best Odessans, the "cream of the crop," she would say in English, were not Russian. "Take Deribas," she said. His mother was the Irish lover of his Spanish father. And they named a street after him.

She wanted water. She bought two bottles and handed one to Oleg. He handed it back. She handed it to him. He handed it back. He didn't want to sweat in front of her. He wanted to impress her by being a dry creature of the steppe.

There was a transaction. She found enough Russian to ask, *Where's the Opera Theater?* She only needed to remember three words: *where, opera,* and *theater.* She could even get away with using the more concise *where Opera?* Full shopping bags draped over both his arms, her Odessan interlocutor lifted his burden to hand to her. While she took and held these bags, the Odessan interlocutor brought his shoulders up as if to hug himself. It wasn't a hug though. It was a shrug. It was a shrug topped off with a stuck out chin. No need to translate that.

Back then, in 2000, they sat in a cafe called "Les Observateurs de la Rue" in the *City Park.* The waitress, after a long look at Sandra, asked "English?" and returned with a menu Sandra could read. She knew the word for what she wanted: *"Pivo."*

Sandra asked Oleg to photograph her in front of a bronze chair. It is a monument to Ilf and Petrov, authors of *The Twelve Chairs.* That Fall was the second one during which boy hustlers began appearing in *City Park.* These boys carried animals on their arms. One offered an iguana, one was draped by a large snake, probably a python, and a little boy nestled a chinchilla. The one with the python draped it over Sandra's shoulders. "You want picture?" She moved, the python moved too, only tighter around the nape of her neck. The boy snapped a Polaroid. The python tightened. "Not move," the boy warned. If she moved too much, if they took too many pictures, it would be ruined. Oleg knew these boys and their racket. He rushed forward, so she could escape the animal photographers.

Another bronze statue — of a man who resembled Yeltsin, she told him — sat on a bench. She sat beside him. What was she doing here? It felt unnatural. She shouldn't be here, Oleg thought. Women, blondes and jet-black brunettes, waify women, strutted past. Oleg was tired of such women. He wanted an *Amerikanka* like Galya was now. Boys stopped girls to talk to them, and the girls followed the boys. Two policemen stalked past, skinny. Their uniforms hung hollow from their collar bones as if inside were only their spines. These were not cops. They were kids. It's a small city. Sandra thought she knew it. Two men, one with an accordion and one with a gapped smile, began to play a song. Music is universal language, mathematics. The pair played a mournful, beautiful melody. Something about it resembled the rise up the hill of the place and, after that, the flatness of the steppe. It was as if, for a second, Sandra remembered something about the place where she was born, something beyond what the names of things were. It was something about the smell. Was there a fragrance to the white acacia trees? The begonias on the lamp posts?

Before he suggested they head home to "rest," it started to rain like the punchline of a great joke. It started to pour. The light softened into a vulnerable quiver. Next came pellets of hail the size of gumballs. She bowed to the weather and rushed along with the crowd, which scattered in every direction. He jumped the little iron fence along the pathway of the park. Her cheeks stung where the hail struck. He pivoted on the lawn, pointed to a tree, and ran toward it at the same time. It wouldn't shelter them, even though they could huddle, even kneel there.

The hail stopped after a couple minutes. The clouds passed. The sun returned. Upswells of steam rose from the ground. They looked at each other, tried to laugh.

"Do-MOI."

For some reason no cars stopped when he stuck out his hand. They had to take a *marshrutka*, a minibus, home. On this *marshrutka*, a little boy spoke English with his mother. The mother shushed him and herself said in quiet, accented English, "You should speak Russian." The boy switched. A woman in a babooshka boarded the minibus. Oleg stood to give up his seat. "*Spasibo, dorogoi,*" the *babushka* said before she fell into his place. Such respect for women in this foreign country! People handed money to each other to pass frontward to the driver. They left through the back door. Others filed in at the front. Like all of them, Sandra closed it in.

The bus strained, the heat clung, pawed at everybody on the *marshrutka*. Oleg closed his eyes. He rode over water, and under the water was Galya's face, lost to him forever, a pale stone staring up. Abruptly, a voice said, "*Allyo?*"

Back in the apartment, they could be alone. Zina was out. He took down a bottle from the kitchen cabinet. Cognac. Or, perhaps, Bessarabian wine. Only, if somebody says Bessarabia, they sound as if they came from no later than 1930. He cleared his throat more times than necessary, which would be even only once, as he showed her the bottle. "*Na-leet tebye?*" He took down two glasses. "Put?" He held a glass out to her.

"Put," she said with a nod.

"*Da?*" He held the bottle out. She nodded. "*Nyet?*" She nodded again. He set the glasses of cognac down. They sat across from one another. He lifted his glass and turned his elbow so that he held the drink with a level forearm. "*Da-vai-te, vui-peem,*" he enunciated. She lifted her glass in the same way. "*Na brudershaft,*" he said.

She recognized the German word, *Bruderschaft*. "Die Bruderschaft." Over his shoulder, the sun set. "Beautiful."

"Booty-fall," he said. He looked back. "Ah. *Za-kat. Zakat* bootyfall."

She pointed at the embroidered tablecloth. "Beautiful."

He frowned. "Booty-fall? *Skatert?*" His finger ticked back and forth between the table cloth and the window, beyond which was the sunset. "Booty-fall *znachit krasivaya.*" His eyes narrowed. "*Ti,*" here it came, "booty-fall." It clearly ruined everything for her, all his charm. Even though they barely spoke the same language. "*Da. Ti krasivaya.*" He tapped the tablecloth as if to draw luck from the wood beneath. "*Ti krasivaya.*"

She did not understand. The cognac probably felt like a sharp-bladed luge in her unaccustomed stomach. Or maybe that's only what he imagined. All the same, that was it for him. "*Ti krasivaya,*" she tried to tell him.

"*Ya? Spasibo.*" He laughed at her. It was all disgusting. He slapped his knees. "*En-da.*" She had no idea what that meant. He recited the great Russian poet, Pushkin, "*Ya vas liubil.*" She did not understand shit.

He made a little burp, looked at his penis. She was all of a sudden "incredibly tired."

"Good night," she said. He didn't say it back to her in her or his language. Sandra, the *Amerikanka*, couldn't save him.

EIGHTEEN

ZINKA

Valinka called her. Her papa was still out at Volodya's. She invited Valinka over, stepped out to buy a bottle of vodka for his visit, and had returned by the time he arrived.

There was definitely something wrong. After several sips, poured by Valinka, drinks which cascaded down her throat as if the vodka was eager to come in from the cold, Zina was prepared. He raised a toast to the Ukrainian Spring. Right before her eyes rolled, making Valinka go out of sight, he looked into them. He drank another glass, poured and drank another. She poured, drank. The vodka made her more prepared. When she stood up to fetch items from the refrigerator, she again felt his gaze. She had thought she could say anything, especially in front of him. Her tongue was petrified. And his gaze was a pressure in the air. His gaze was gravity that drew her toward the engine of his imagination and tongue. Seated like a towel drying on a chair, he gazed at her. Without taking her eyes off his face, she poured him more vodka, which he drank without taking his eyes off hers. The whole room watched her as if a decentralized drone radiated from the entirety of their surroundings. It was because she let him fuck her. She wondered now if that was how he would put it. At once she understood what might have gone through Galya's mind when Zina's papa had made some kind of move, said some piece of sleaze to Galya. Even if his words had not been a bad joke, even if they had been devastating, the one time in his life Zina's papa had executed an anecdote well, she knew that Galya's reaction had all the same been a shrug, the words to herself, *Why not? You could do worse, girl.*

Some vodka dribbled from the corner of Valinka's mouth and caught the light like a spider's eye. He kissed away the vodka on his fingers, eyes still locked on hers. Locked. Her. In the catacombs, she had said some word, invoked some power from within him that made him think he knew all that was inside her because he had entered. That was a problem. She shifted her glass between hands and took a breath, about to tell a story. Wary of her papa, even though he wasn't there, she spoke English, "When we were in catacombs, it was your first time. Not mine."

"That depends on what you mean by 'first time,'" he said, rubbing his face, covering his eyes. His own words appeared to have confused him.

"You want to play with words?" she asked. Yes. That was the answer, she told herself. Her papa's solution to problems was usually to take out pen and paper. One New Years, he had handed out pen and paper and suggested they write in the Zaum style of poetry, where you were supposed to use sounds as symbols, make up words. Since she could not tell Valinka about what happened, she took out paper and a pen and wrote down a poem in the Zaum style:

Dere down, down dere
Dip, dist ants, verb, naked,
Taken, take, exchange but taken
Crumpled, death, thought, SM, A LL
Not necessary, Spanish nothing, not nothing is something.
Not nothing is everything.

When she was finished, she said, "I am the poet but don't know it. *Ili.*" Valinka took the paper, read it with audible breaths, sounding out the morphemes, and lay it down again. She had retaken power. That was clear by the way his gravity had inverted and become a swallowing silence around him. Finally, she had lead him to shut up. She had still not told him what happened.

Maybe this will work, she wrote in a black, strapped notebook given to her when she was a teenager, when it had been considered a top-tier luxury and she had been afraid to write in it except her name. Her papa had joked that now, with her name in it, it was less valuable. She had written her name by the light of a candle wedged into a bullet casing from the Great Patriotic War. She had lit this candle, sat, and begun to write:

This wound still aches. Before sunrise on June 19, 2003, an older boy named Anton and I stole a boat along one of the canals in Peresyp. It was on the other side of a pontoon bridge. It seems people didn't expect anybody to want to cross the bridge or to steal it. We promised ourselves we would return it the next night. Whoever boat it was might never notice that it was missing. On the water, nothing was visible unless it moved, because stirred bubbles trap light. Currents crossed, overlapped, licked the boat. But even when it was calm and quiet as the dead, I could hear the salt.

We paddled across the main port. The rusted sky brimmed on the water to the east. It was calm, as usual. Anton took pieces of a feather and tied it around a lure, something to whisper in a fish's ear, attract her. He dropped the rope down and let it dance, up and down, as if to underwater music. I ate a beet and listened to myself chew. While fishing, it's wrong to pay attention. Here's one, I told Anton. In fifth class, to Abramovich was posed the following math question — if you have six beets, and you give half to Katya, how many do you have left? Five and a half, says Abramovich. Anton didn't laugh.

The line became as tight as a throat when it sings. I helped him pull it up. A mackerel. I imagined the mackerel staring up at the boy in the boat on the other side of the surface as if she could hear her voice and wanted to talk to her. Then, thoughtlessly, she took a bite of something to eat, an easy offering at a time in the early morning when she was hungry. Whatever she swallowed wrenched the voice out of her. But she caught on and held her mouth closed because she knew this would take her to the other side. When she came to the other side, she heard nothing. She never heard the boy even though she called out to him before. If fish could dream, a nightmare would destroy her desire to break through the surface. But she only wanted to talk to the boy, not listen. Now she can never return. Now, through pain, she understands. The fish lay there, her mouth pulsing. I watched the fish even though I only wanted to eat her. I wanted her to tell me what it meant, my hunger for her. This mystery was what kept me from devouring the fish before she died. The mouth opened and closed. I wonder if this happened before, if this was a dream of another meal of fish I ate along my way. I wonder if it was a nightmare. I wished health on her, the fish. I wished for her to live longer. She talked in a language nobody understood. Except other fish. I collected myself and smashed her on the gunwale. One eye was still whole, but she was dead.

To the south of the city's main port, cliffs along the beach lead up to Park Shevchenko. The red sunrise would soon touch the beach and rise up the cliffs to the arcade of the old fortress along the top edge, where it would pass under its arches. Waves crashed against the high shores of Odessa to smash the fortress wall, to smash all that was left of the city. The sea slipped back down out of the awkward bow the cliffs made it do.

We brought the boat close to the concrete sea wall. I climbed out with my bag, and together we flipped the boat and waited for a wave to push it up, pulled it onto the sea wall, and slid it across the top. When it was in the water on the other side, we flipped it and saw that the gunwales were badly scraped. I hadn't heard anything. We brought it to shore, a slab on Great Fountain Beach. The sun had come up. We climbed into a drainage pipe and, with some grass and shards of wood and a cigarette lighter, I started a fire. Anton took some chestnut leaves that had blown onto the beach. I cleaned the fish like papa taught me. I put it in the wet leaf and lay it in the early coals of the fire. Who would ask for more than this? That's it. I was done.

When fish die, they come to the surface. When fish cross the surface, they must die.

We stepped lightly on the grass bordering a path. We didn't want Odessa to hear us. We kept our faces buried in our shirts, greeted nobody. It's not the Odessan way. When I stopped shrugging my shoulders, the smell of my clothing fell away too. The smell of grass announced itself, seconded by the spray of the sea. Up ahead on the seaside path was the stucco wall of a dacha. As the path slipped and crumbled over itself upward, the path became bordered by bricks with points turned skyward. Along that wall, from the smoldering light of a window, a song was playing, "Dark night, bullets flying in the steppes, only wind blows in the wires, and stars dimly twinkle/ in the dark night, you, my love, aren't sleeping..." Over the wall, in the garden, aster, chrysanthemum, and spider lily bloomed. Galya taught me those.

Anton wanted to snooze in a dacha in Arkadia where a little garden scents each breath. He wanted to drink sassafras tea. I was sated. The last rumbling trolley shrieked before retreating down Big Fountain. It'll switch over to French Boulevard, passing mansions, until it almost reaches the Lanzheron stairs, where it will slow to a whisper into the soft seashell ear of a whore.

I sang a song that my grandmother sang.

Women from southwest of the city arrived humming. As the sun rose, their hum became song. They all looked the same, all dragging an invisible barge behind them. I asked one, "Where's 'hedgehoggies?'" That was the secret name of the entrance to the catacombs along the shore. I heard that these women knew. In whispers like spiders' web across my face, she told me, "Who are you? You should go." But I didn't move. She sucked her lip a little bit. "When you pass the Big Fountain, go ashore at Halkovyi Beach. Climb along the wall now, while the tide's out. There's a hole where you have to climb up about five meters. You'll have to slide on your butt. Then you'll stand and walk, then you'll crawl again. Don't ever write this down."

Anton and I did as she said. We floated to Halkovyi. We climbed along the side of the wall, entered the chamber. At first Anton tried to climb. I couldn't, so he climbed down. He pushed me from underneath. Then I could climb on my own. There was a hole in the side, through which I crawled. I had to take off my backpack. When the tunnel became large enough that we were able to stand inside, we started to run, holding the cigarette lighter in front of us. The rock was soft as shell, firm but tender, and I ran my hand along it, rumbling, like the fur of a gentle, tender beast, who sleeps underground.

If you say you will do something dangerous and romantic and stupid, you must do it and go as far as you can. Although it was clear people were here before, we weren't afraid. I wasn't. Earlier somebody set up a tiny kitchen and a small bed. Anton even drank some of the salty water. He said, "Drink it fast. Don't let it touch the tongue." But I didn't drink. He said he saw an albino fish in here once. There were signals on the walls. Anton said they corresponded to the streets of the city itself.

We lay there, chatting. He said, "My girl speaks English. I should speak English."

"I'm not your girl. Why speak English?"

"Why do you speak it?" He smiled like he had suddenly taken out a knife.

"My mama went to America," I said. That always shut him up even though we expected his parents to croak at any time.

"So you want to be one of them, an American? You can't be American, Zinka. Americans buy a car every day. You never rode in one."

"I rode in one."

"When?"

"A couple of times."

He laughed, and it was like a machine gun. "That doesn't count."

"Yes! I could be an American if my mom could."

"You're wrong."

"You're wrong."

He shrugged. "Means one of us is crazy."

"Means you are," I said. "Why would you learn English, then, if not to be American?"

"To serve."

"To serve as who? The director of communication? Of a factory in Naval?" I hit him hard. I shouldn't have done that. Even if he let me. I should have felt responsible for that little violence in that pocket space where horror gathered. "What do you know about this space? Tell me history, the history of Odessa."

"Odessa began in 1789."

"I know that. But it's older," I said.

He rolled his eyes. "This is where the partisans were. There's a passage to Tairovsky."

"Where I'll end up one day," I said.

"Where we'll all fall one day. But don't talk like that, dear. There's a passage into the city. But that's blocked, I think. There was a small group of partisans. The commander was Lazarov."

"I heard of Lazarov," I told him. I turned my back to him.

"In the direction toward Tairovsky, there's a radio. It works with a crank. If you turn it, you can talk to ghosts."

"Which language do they speak?" I asked.

"They speak like us, dear. You can talk to ghosts, Zinka. They'll say, 'Don't walk away from the apparatus. Now you'll receive instructions.' And you'll sit there. And you'll wait." He was quiet. I turned, sat up. His eyes were closed. Then that smile. "You'll hear children laughing." I hit him again, harder. It was the kind of blow not easily forgiven.

"With you I can laugh. I can't laugh with my papa. He doesn't laugh. Even when he jokes. He's so broken."

"Your papa?"

Anton rolled and stood up. He went into one of the tunnels. I heard him step slowly, softly. The step became softer. The single flame from the lighter became nothing more than a jewel of light that retreated. I thought I would have to follow his sound alone, its procession down the passage. But he began to light candles there, *tiny burning eyes set at various places on little shelves in the shell-rock walls. It was so stupid and romantic. I didn't yet know that it was dangerous.*

"Eh, Anton!" I yelled. I should find him. I should ask him to apologize. It's simply a word, he'd probably say.

But I used words. They came from my mouth. That mouth he covered when I entered the darkness where he went. That was the worst of it. I had a voice with which I navigated the world. With it, I told my desires and fears. It was my sound, and he snuffed it with a dirty, sweaty palm. To me that was death. I used words. No more.

He knelt and pulled at my pants. He took down my underwear and kissed my pussy. He spoke the English letter L, where you must touch the top of your mouth, L with a soft sign. He spoke this letter into my pussy. He pulled at my hand. And that's when I tried to use words again. That's when I knew that the silence damaged my voice. Because I said, "Ne nado." I said it with a gentle tone. I said that, and I clasped his fingers in my own. "Ne nado," I said again. I clasped his hand again.

When I look it up on the internet, "Ne Nado" is a phrase that can mean, literally, "not necessary," made up of the negative "ne," "which in English is not or non- or un-," and *"nado," "which is more 'necessary' than* nuzhno." *You understand? I must translate it. It can be misused.*

But it is universally accepted as more of a command. "Don't." An Odessan knows this. Anton was a true Odessan.

I also told him I was uncomfortable. I couldn't move there.

But what he did, he did. "You can't unring a bell," my girl in Detroit said once. It can't be undone. Maybe an American would think it could. Maybe Galya. But not an Odessitka. Not I.

We left the catacombs. We left the cave. Our black blindness became white. Echoed, enclosed sound became absorbed by the wind of the beach which would sweep away even machine gun laughter.

Halkovyi Beach was empty before. Now a wedding was taking place there. Men, women, boys, and little girls were there, all dressed well. But there was no groom, and all that was left of the bride was a white headband and veil, flailing against the wind. The guests' skins weren't dusty with cave dirt. But each of them lost their voice too.

They said nothing as we proceeded through the only open space to the position on the rock where the white veil was. We proceeded past the makeshift veil. We climbed a path up to the cliff. We came to the top. For a moment, the wind died. I looked down. It was my hand in Anton's. I looked back down the path, down at the beach, to the cave. The girls from the wedding climbed the rocks toward its entrance. I saw one go in. I could swear I heard her scream, but how could I hear anything with that wind?

NINETEEN

VALENTINE

May Day was upon us. My money was reduced almost exclusively to the kind that clinks. I had found a hostel in the city to stay, and it was costing all my remaining cash. A woman, who had said I reminded her of her son, had stolen the emergency credit card my mom had given me. I was trying to negotiate with the hostel owner to stay longer. My visa would soon expire. I still hadn't heard from Zina. The plunge of the end was audible in my mind.

I called her on the hostel phone. If I was about to leave Odessa, I had to talk to her first. "It is good to hear your voice," she said. "I thought you hate me."

I waited, unafraid of silence between us now. I heaved my heart to my mouth. *I tried to leave. I couldn't.*

"Ha ha," she said. "You are mine."

"Yes, it would seem so," I said.

"I want to see you. Please come."

When I hung up, the hostel owner was staring me down. *You say you don't have money. But you speak English. It's impossible you don't have money.*

Within ten minutes, I was out the door with my backpack in hand. As I put it on, I bowed goodbye to Zhenya, the owner of the hostel. He said, *Remember the rule. Don't believe, don't be afraid, don't ask anything. Our ancestors* — he had accepted me as Ukrainian, for which I was eternally grateful — *starved. Those who survived the war began to nibble. They nibbled a little bit extra every day while the situation improved. They even put on a few pounds. They prob-*

ably were about the size of an average American, not a fat one. In their fat was stored the memory of the depravity of the war. Now...now, if it will be bad again, if people will be hungry again, they will burn their fat, open the memories stored there, memories of war, like in Eastern Ukraine. But that won't come to Odessa. I took the man at his word, thanked him for his wisdom, and left the hostel. I had a feeling that some drama would play out once I reached Zina. I thought that the best case scenario was that she would finally decide to be in love with me. The worst case scenario was that she would tell me she never wanted to see me again. Either way, I would be able to sit with her one more time, maybe to touch her hand. I would hear her voice. I would have traveled across the world to hear her voice.

As I came to *Old Bazaar Square,* a Roma person spotted me and wandered forward as if I was a magnet that attracted her. In a mysterious whisper, the spectral woman told me, *I can predict the future.* As she spoke, she covered her mouth as if something would escape. A bitter, pickled taste filled my mouth. The Roma woman said, *What was, was. What will be, will be. Don't fear death. Don't live in this world.*

She laid her palm out.

When speaking with the Roma people, I had heard Zina say, *Yes, "madam-s."* This strange formal Russian marked her as intelligent, as somebody not a tourist, as an Odessitka. I wanted to give off the same air.

"*Da. Madam-s,*" I said.

The Roma woman turned her cheek. I could smell that she wasn't wearing deodorant. Her voice took on a depth as if she were yawning while she spoke. *Ah, you're clever people, I reckon.* She had used the *vous* with me. But she had also said *people* as if I was more than one. She appeared to grow as she said, *You don't need my predictions. But, remember my words! Tomorrow, the second of May will be an evil day!* After saying that, she shrunk. *Until then, many blessings to you.* She left, and around her former place was a small circle of emptiness, rumbling with the wind.

I still had a day.

When I did see Zina, there was something wrong, a silence that pressed between us. When she spoke, her voice had turned, sounded more girlish, which was more frightening than her usual sneer. I would never be to her what she was to me. It felt as if this strangeness would remain until death. Sitting with her, drinking *Bready Gift*, I became so drunk that I fell asleep in the bed where I had slept before.

When I woke up in the morning, she was standing over me. Seeing that I was awake, she opened a notebook and showed me a text written in Russian, in her handwriting.

When Zina came back to the room and saw that I had put the notebook down, she asked, "You read?"

"I read," I said.

"Well?"

I could feel my face crumpling like paper. My voice tapered into a boy's whine to say, "Am I like Anton?"

"No," she answered.

You quit men because of that?

More or less. "Da."

I never felt more at a loss for words. I wanted to hide my face, to cry. Not even to cry, to weep. Something came to me to say.

I'll translate it. It will be in my language.

"No," she said. "I want it to stay in the language I wrote."

"There's nothing I can say. Nothing I can do."

"Nope." She shrugged.

"I," and it came to me that her father might hear. I began in Russian. I switched to English so that he wouldn't understand, "*Tvoi*...Does your dad know? Shouldn't we be quiet?"

"My papa, he in the *Jewish Hospital*."

"Oh my God! Why?"

"What? You gonna save him?" Zina waited. "No." The pitch of her voice dropped down again. "Maybe you can heal him. He has

the wound from radiation. He worked on a generator. It happen
to him when he go for your money from the man who stole it.
Here it is. Your three hundred *hryven. Vot.*" She handed me a stack
of Ukrainian cash. I took it and closed my eyes as tightly as possible. She said, "There was," *what's it called,* "*Strontsky* Ninety. Now
he's sick. He jokes that when your condition's nice, it means you
close to death. Hospice is best, he says. I shush him. Then he start
to talk about my grandmama. I point my finger upward at god.
But this mean only to be quiet. I don't let the priest at the hospital
through the door."

"I'm sorry, Zinochka," I said.

"That sounds weird from you. Zinochka. You will come to see
him at the hospital? If you heal him, I will love you forever." She
began to speak in a rambling monologue, so bizarre that I had to
write it down. *In my dreams, when my papa comes, he speaks English.
That's how I know they're dreams. It defies the laws of who he is. Even if
he understood English, I think he would have forbidden it. This pre-Babel
state, it's not him. I'm not talking about the condition before the Odessan writer, Isaak Babel, of course. I'm talking about something Biblical,
about which my papa knows little, being a typical atheist "sovok." Pre-
Babel is the time before languages. They so violently divide us. He speaks
Russian, Ukrainian, and, most of all, Odessan. But he doesn't speak English, no matter how hard English tries to lift his tongue up.*

Her father hadn't even wanted to eat the meatballs she had
made, which she handed to me in a crumpled napkin. He was already tired of the books she had brought, the ones he'd salvaged
from a derelict library. *He's dying too young. But people die young all
the time. When did his papa die? His papa was already gone while he
grew up. At least, I had a papa.* It wasn't the first time I had heard
her rambling. As usual, all I could say was, "Da," at several points.
He won't die. This is what he did to Galya. Her tone had dropped. *He
worried whether he left his young life behind when he married her. This he
worried about until she left him. Then he had his life without her again.
He could see his friends whenever he wanted. He could do whatever he*

wanted. Except for me, of course. I was there to keep him from liquor and goulash for every meal.

I tried to disagree with what she had said before, *He'll live.*

The argument had already passed. *He'll live? You're an American. To you, everything is through pink glasses.*

And to you through black ones. But I don't blame you.

You can't blame me. And my glasses aren't black. They're the many colors of the butterfly's wing. You have to be a realist.

I am a realist. Radiation poisoning isn't going to kill him. They caught it in time. He'll live longer. It's the ongoing exposure that kills you.

I slowly gnawed a meatball down to nothing.

The ongoing exposure to what? If it's not the radiation, it's this place, Odessa, Ukraine. It'll kill him. It'll kill you too if you stay. Zina punctuated her speech with laughter, and even though the meatball she had put in her mouth muffled it, the sound almost made me cry.

I'm surprised you know "radiation poisoning" and "ongoing exposure." So many words you've acquired for yourself here. Enough? Between chews she asked, *You know the joke about the kids whose school was under renovation? During that time, their inventory of words increased.*

Why? This question proved that I was still not an Odessan by language.

The workers curse so much...

Ah, I understood. Funny.

Yes. Funny. Neither of us laughed. *That friend of his, Volodya, came to Echo Archive and demanded we give him our computers. He's a separatist, a nationalist. I should kill him, but I don't have the time.*

What's going on with that? This question sounded blasphemous to me, an American question.

They're setting up tents in Kulikovo Field, by the Trade Unions House. Then, there's supposed to be a counter-demonstration on Transfiguration.

Oh. You're saying that people here don't always agree? I hoped she would catch the joke. It would redeem me.

It did not. And what I wanted to say in Russian didn't come together fast enough. Zina stood to go and read to her father

197

even though he was still asleep. *At least I returned. Not like mama. If she returned, I could heal.* She shrugged again, and my heart did so with her. *We're alike, Valinka. But between your glasses and my glasses there are two big differences.*

Not only one big difference. It's as if there are layers of difference. She was circling the wagons. I was on the wrong side.

At the hospital, when her father saw Zina, he said, *I'm not dying, Zina. You understand, the closest I came to death was when they wouldn't let me in to see you born.* I stepped through the door, and he bundled up, turned away from me as if I had stung him. Zina made little legs with her fingers and pointed me toward the door, which she shut once I stepped out.

In the end, I was here for Zina. If I could help her father, well, maybe she really meant what she had said. His suffering only mattered to me through her as a translation. In the same way that I only cared for him through her, I wanted the whole world to care for Zina through me. I wanted to translate her suffering into a language that would reach and convince all that here was a woman they must heed.

She stepped out at one point and told me not to accompany her. She needed some time to think. I stayed behind, thinking maybe she would come back and want me to translate her suffering. Lost in such thoughts, I must not have noticed that somebody had entered her father's room. The door was open. What was once Zina's peacoat hung from a chair like it was a curtain, a border. Zina and I were on different sides of its thin, silky lining. The peacoat was one of those subtle and supposedly insignificant details which continue to come up in human memory, where they have so permanently impressed themselves during the most important events. Details like these include a madeleine, the cork lying on the floor after the final bottle of champagne, a certain trio of cards in the deck, acacia leaves and cigarette butts, glistening scores of scar tissue on the forearm near the wrist. They can be as trivial or as noisy with meaning as sex in a communal apartment. This pea-coat had gone to the West and become tainted. It was the *neumest-nost*, the out-of-placeness, of it that lingered even after the pea-coat had returned to Odessa.

In that chair sat the junkman, Volodya. Having seen Zina step out, he must have come in. Visible within the space between door and frame, he and her father sat speaking what I couldn't hear. Her father was colorless, already white through to the bone. Zina's father and Volodya were reliving the past, two sailors hunched so close they must have been either plotting or trading puckered kisses.

My curiosity wasn't enough that I would confront Volodya. I sat down again and waited until Volodya left the room. When he stalked out, I entered. Her father was asleep. I saw how Zina resembled him somewhat, the darker features, the upturned nose and the cheekbones. For a second, there was Zina as I had never seen her before, wounded, vulnerable. He opened his eyes, and Zina was gone. He cleared his throat, and said, *What do you want?* I sat against the peacoat. It poked me. I had to sit forward, elbows on my knees, to hear him. *You must help me escape this place. There are microbes, sicknesses in the air here.*

You should stay. They heal you here. As if I was speaking to Zina, I used the *tu* with him. It was the only time I ever did so.

He let the air settle. *I must go to Kulikovo Field. There will be a meeting.*

I don't think, I said, lost searching for the next words while he crushed his pillow and I tried to help lift him up.

Light as a feather, he was as loud as a bird of prey. *Well, that's your problem. I do think*, he said, punctuating the last two words. He rearranged his nest of sheets. *So, listen attentively.* He whispered about how I should help him walk to the door and sit on the trolley that would take him to Kulikovo Field. *There I must chat with Volodya. He's a fool, but I must go to him. There will be a fight. Maybe I can stop him. If I can stop him, I can stop many.*

I wanted to tell him how to escape through the catacombs beneath. I thought my Odessan savvy would impress him. Instead I joked, *You'll fight somebody? I don't think so, pop.* I made a reminder to myself to tell Zina how I had used that Ukrainian word, pronounced "bot." *At the moment, I myself could make you fall.* He glared at me. Around the edges of those black pebbles, deep within, I could see the murmur of a tear. Finally, this man was revealing fear before me. If he was revealing fear, that meant maybe Zina would too. I shrugged, backed away, afraid to spoil such a victory. He lifted up in bed and craned his neck to watch me retreat. The growing distance would narrow the pitch of his voice, make it higher and more focused.

In the hall, I thought of shouting *victory*. I meekly said, "*Pobyeda!*" so that nobody would hear. It would still be the hubris of an American winner, not the fried gritty howl of a hoarse Soviet victor. It would have been better to shout my "*Pobyeda!*" in the face of my own father, not Zina's. All the same, celebratory noise overwhelmed my head after I had witnessed that physical dressing down of this poor man.

It was this celebratory noise that drowned out the minor, mumbled negotiation between a male nurse, who entered after me, and Zina's father. The nurse was a guy my age. He was a guy who might want to make some extra money, take his woman for a night out, buy her some ice cream, something extravagant. All it would cost him was some convenient neglect, a momentary oversight, a blind spot in time during which that Soviet crow whose skin was flaking off could slip out through the little used corner exit, which was not alarmed despite a sign on the door stating that it was.

When I came back in to his room with a glass of water, Zina's father was already gone. Zina wouldn't love me. She'd kill me.

TWENTY

ZINA

The Second of May, 2014, it was a little cloudy in Odessa. Zina always loved clouds, how their light made visible the ongoing tremble of the world. After she left her papa, Zina wanted only to move. There had always been a need within her to leave the place where she was and return to hear it for the first time.

She boarded one of Odessa's many microbus routes. She didn't know which one. She picked randomly and found herself on a *marshrutka* that took her away from the city center, away from American tourists, further, even from other post-Soviet people touring Odessa, further, into parts of the city where haggling is demanded by people's budgets. She picked her nose, discreetly. Hope had crested, spritzed her face. Immediately, she knew it was the kind of hope that is a rabid lie, feverish, evaporating along with sweat. All the same, it healed her somewhat, touched her forehead, her chin, lifted it like the fingers of a mother. All the same motherless, maybe she could still love him. Even though she was sitting, she felt as light as the butterfly, throwing herself — since butterflies are feminine in her language — against the window. She flew out of the open sunroof, opened her wings and was free above Odessa. The smell of cotton candy rose from Park Shevchenko. There, not far below her, was that turning *devil's wheel*. There was the Opera Theater. The Black Sea was as flat as a pane laid on the floor. For a moment, this butterfly forgot she wasn't a bird. She kept going, her torso as black as that vastness, which did not swallow her, only lightly kissed her with puckered waves before she herself plunged in.

Tucked into her seat, Zina let the hope recede like the wave it was. *What's wrong with the life of an Odessitka? I can buy an apartment here for $200,000. How much am I short? Ten dollars.* She even laughed at her own joke. A man saw her smile, and he sighed.

She was only a butterfly. Still, her death became an absence, a wound in the cloth of the world. The woven order came undone. Sometimes people patch such wounds with recycled textures, familiarities, the same old jokes. For those who look closely at the weavings of the world, return is impossible. Abandon all hope, said graffiti in Detroit. That was for a butterfly. What about mass violence, like what was happening in Kiev, when the fabric unravels in several places at once and becomes like the view from underneath a holey cloak, looking like the night sky? If Valinka asked her which side she was on with regard to Ukraine, she would say, *I don't know.* Even if he asked in English, she would answer that way. She would gesture, palms up, at all that surrounds them, Odessa, Odessans, the *produkty* in their kitchen windows, the *shtuki* in their stores. Valinka would say that he would like to enter those homes. Only the stores let him enter. He wants to see Odessa, to hear her. He wants her voice to speak from within him. *But you're not Odessan*, she would tell him. *It's a luxury not to be lost in the ongoing whirlwind of violence.*

When Valinka saw her approaching, he hopped to his feet. *He left. Your papa left.*

Without responding, she rushed toward the emergency exit. This act was, after all, an emergency.

Now instead of the path of the butterfly, she began to narrate to herself the path of her papa. In his peacoat and with his unbelted pants clutched in a fist, he must have treaded on flip flops to the corner emergency exit. Flip flops. No alarm sounded. Her own step is faster, more steady and stable. He took a left, northwest on *Meat Eaters' Street*, in the direction of the *Old Horse Market*. She does the same. When she passes the market, she hears the parrots there speaking Yiddish. Her papa was falling. Anybody would, wearing flip flops. What's important is where exactly. The parrots of *Old Horse Market* say, "*Helfe. Helfe mir.*"

He must have taken a trolley for a couple clanging stops. Clutching the pole, she gathers her spite, like he must have. It always helps to concentrate a scrappy power. With this power he must have removed his feeble self from the trolley only a few blocks from where he climbed on, where she herself leaps from the trolley. The concrete is uneven. It always has been, her whole life through to the end of the Soviet era, through the breakdown of the Nineties, into the sensitive teenage years of Ukraine, the Aughts, and now to the era of Maidan.

She implores this place, her oldest girlfriend, to help her echo-locate her papa. Instead of helping, an Odessan hums an old ditty, an ex-sailor's, who salutes what happened in Crimea. He knows, all the same, that an Odessitka takes her own route. The ex-sailor, a Soviet patriot, would rather slobber over the feet of a man bald as Lenin than say *I obey!* to a small-time "junta," his word, not Zina's.

As she strides toward Kulikovo, Zina sees a troop of ultras passing in front of the train station. Their shoulders are draped in Ukrainian flags, underneath which are some *Chernomorets*—the Odessan soccer team—t-shirts but also some from *Metallist*—Kharkov's team—too. Each carries throbbing fists with rags twisted around them. A teenager on a bench sets down bottles with rags out their necks, Molotov Cocktails. Her smile, as she twists the rags through the bottlenecks, is like a stifled scream.

Zina ducks her head as she sees, astride a bicycle, a boy with a cobblestone unmistakable as one of those that make up *Deribas Street*. All his life he has known that there was only one use for these cobblestones. He never dared himself until this moment to drape from his bicycle and pick one up to throw.

Odessans shout *Where are you from?* at the Odessan Police.

A man wanders among the chestnut trees and ambulances, holding out his hands like overturned chairs and screaming,

We're all Odessans! Odessans look at him as if to say duh. Somebody punched him in the gut. Even though he didn't think it hurt that much, there's a metallic taste in his mouth.

A body in the street flaps its arm as if waving you over. It wants to tell you an anecdote. Tell you the truth, the arm is moving because somebody is performing the pulmonary pumps of CPR on the torso to which it's attached. He won't make it, his anecdote will go unheard.

Anecdote: there's a dead body shot in the street. What? You think that's news? That's not new, so it's not news.

An Odessitka makes her way onto Kulikovo Field. The tent city there is in cracked and tangled piles. A barricade in the shape of a sickle hunkers in front of the *Trade Unions House*. There is Volodya, gazing out, doing his best impression of Stalin. She pivots toward him. At the barricade, she shouts that she's the daughter of Oleg Bondarenko. They make an opening for her, and she hurries through. Volodya has already climbed the steps into the *Trade Unions House*, where she presumes her papa is.

In the backseat of an abandoned, unclaimed Volga sedan lies a gym bag. Inside that gym bag are a soldering iron, a hacksaw, bronze, nitrate, and a blowtorch. The car next to it was the site of some fondling between a couple who were never able to consummate their relationship.

Long Slavic legs sprint onto Kulikovo Field, stomp on canvas tents, topple slipshod barricades. Cigarette-burned, scarred forearms clutch two-by-fours. Odessans lob rocks at other Odessans, at themselves, as if they wished the rocks were grenades. As you do in any relationship, Odessans built a barricade between themselves. It is rigged with sandbags and plasterboard. Now Odessans are setting it on fire.

Zina was climbing stairs. Other Odessans climb, duck under open windows, hug walls built by ancestors. The blast of the blowtorch draws beads of fear from their pores. A boy shouts, *They're regularly dropping fire from the roof*, a warning, a little bit of advice, five kopecks, take or leave it. A man nearby fires a pistol at that roof and those open windows. *Kokteily molotova* and petrol bombs make violent traffic through the air, robin-red flames that flare and fall.

Zina hears Russian, Ukrainian, Odessan. Whatever they speak in Odessa is what is spoken there. She doesn't hear her papa. She keeps expecting to see him shuffle past, his arm akimbo against the wound in his side. She sees men with this grandmotherly posture. They could be any wounded Odessan. Many Odessans limp like he does. The flames roar like the crowd's jeer at the Odessan fool.

The tongue simply flexes its muscle, outlasts everything until everything's ash, climbs from the inside outside and, in the end, chokes an Odessitka with a final rattle. Odessa died. Odessa is dying. Odessa will die. Odessa lived. Odessa is living. Odessa will live. She'll live fantastically.

Odessa is a burned woman burning, her tongue the last of her.

She hears Galya. She didn't know the woman was dead. How else could her mama be here in this burning building? And her mama is speaking English. Her voice sounds as if smoke were burying itself in her throat. The flame, like upward rain, ushers life out of her. Curtains, the fire, close on Odessa's operatic death scene.

Such a drama queen Odessa is.

Zina simply snuck out the stage left door to have a smoke. That was best now. Blow it all out like the drag life was.

"Mama!"

You can understand, of course, how much of a relief it was for Zina to be, all of a sudden, swimming in the Black Sea. She came up for breath, dove, came up, dove again, deeper, came up, her breath almost expired by the time she breached. She dove again, even deeper. She desperately needed to cough, and it's impossible to cough underwater, so she gave in and came to the surface.

She couldn't see the beach anymore, not even the sea wall. There was only water. Her mask must be fogged. She took it off, breathed on it. There was no breath. If there was no breath, it meant there were no longer any words.

TWENTY-ONE

VALYA

When I watched her leave that day, I thought she'd never love me now if something happened to her father. She'd blame me. I would have gone after him myself for her. She was already on the case.

I read that, in times of uncertainty, of mystery about what will happen next, all anybody has is hope, *nadezhda*, a common Russian name. Hope. I thought, if only I could come up with a good joke or anecdote, if only I could get a laugh from her, one that wasn't a result of a mistake in Russian. Maybe not a laugh, if only I could get a nod, or simply a wry little smile, maybe then I could make it work between us. Even though I was worried that she would kill me for not keeping tabs on her father, I busied myself with coming up with a joke to tell her. These thoughts occupied my mind as I walked home. On the street I couldn't understand anything, not a single word anybody spoke. I knew that I had to word this joke in Russian. It would be my swan song.

Having known that Volodya had been in the *Trade Unions Building*, having heard about the fire, I had already begun to word the joke. It occupied my mind. I even wrote it down. I thought this joke would slay. *Guess what?* I'd say, *I think the murder you proposed, to kill Volodya, actually happened yesterday. And you're still innocent! Congratulations!* I would be referring to the news that people had died in the fire in the *Trade Unions Building* in Kulikovo Field. The joke still sounded strange, though. I could already hear Zina snort, could see the bass clef she would trace with her rolling eyes.

But Zina wasn't home. And when her father, when Oleg finally came home, his face told me that she was dead.

Then he told me. *Zina died.* He touched his finger to his lips, and I remembered Zina doing that, the international sign for please shut up. She usually followed with a bright smile, killing with kindness. She must have done that a lot in this place where we now stood. She must have smiled, shrugged, over and over again for years. Eventually, I heard Oleg again. He said, *I never made it to Kulikovo. Collapsed in the Old Horse Market, and they carried me behind a kiosk. There I passed out hearing the jibes of Yiddish parrots. One of them even called me a wacko. It was strange because the last time anybody had called me wacko was the last time I spoke to Zina. We were arguing about the very place, Kulikovo Field, where I wanted to go, the Trade Unions House there, where she died.*

"*It was built in honor of foreign workers, who toiled and suffered for the motherland,*" *I told her. She said,* "*I read witness of the time that it was just an office building for officials. They were known to be especially corrupt.*" "*'Ili.' From where does this gossip come?*" *I asked her because I was offended that Zina thought she knew better.* "*Papa. It's my work.*" "*Well, you're confused. You don't know what you read.*"

"*How can it be more different than what you said? Two big differences,*" *she said.* "*You don't know what you read.*" These words he said sadder than he could have said them at the time. He sobbed. *Her last words to me were,* "*That means one of us is wacko.*" *I told her,* "*That means you are.*" Tears were there, like a bucket of water on top of a door. I was there too. That bucket would remain. At least he let me witness what he did.

After that, whispering what sounded like prayers or incantations to himself, he turned around and walked to his bedroom. Behind the walls of a neighboring apartment, I heard somebody say the one word, "*Ili.*" I waited for my inner Zina to reply.

Oleg had long ago acquired a plot in Tairovsky Cemetery. He'd done so after long ago having attended an Odessan version of a Quaker meeting, made up of people he called the *Dukhobory*. What's important is how, here at this meeting, it was explained to him that he should prepare for death before any journey. He chose to focus on the former part of that statement since he didn't expect ever to journey away from Odessa.

Now there was a use for his plot.

I still had the phone number for Alyosha, the driver who weeks ago had taken me and Zina to visit her grandmother's grave. I called him, and he remembered us and agreed to drive me to Zina's funeral.

For him, it was business as usual. He commented on billboards we passed on the road, *The Party of Regions used to have signs up that said, "Odessa became a city of a million," as if it had never been so before.* He turned into the second gate of the cemetery, *Here that million lie, underground.*

Actually, we should have entered at the third gate, I told him.

Alyosha shrugged.

At the third gate, I stopped to buy flowers from the *babushkas* there, the same ones from whom I'd bought flowers for Zina's grandmother, the same ones who had *swindled* me. In my mind, I used the word Alyosha had used to mean that, literally *blew*. I thought of telling them that I knew they had *blown* me, that now I was buying flowers for that young woman with whom I had come. I thought of starting out by saying, *I already know how much. Thirty-three. No, three hundred three.*

I pointed at the flowers I wanted. She asked for *thirty-three.* I had nothing witty to say, said nothing at all, and set out over the dusty crush toward the sea of graves.

She stopped me. "Eh!"

I turned and saw her eyes. Who had been the last resident of Odessa to make eye contact with me? Zina, of course. I said, *Three hundred three?* It must have been the way I walked.

You're going to leave the English way? Without saying goodbye?

I remembered hearing the Odessan response to this. "*Da*," I said. *The English leave like that. And Odessans...they say goodbye but don't leave.* I awaited her laughter.

She was smiling, even chuckling a little. And, surely out of laughter, a tear appeared on her cheek. The peak of light on its lens quivered, inside it a miniature universe of the world where we stood.

I got the joke.

TWENTY-TWO

During the war bodies hung from lampposts. The cemetery had no purpose. At least it hasn't become that bad yet. Trucks riding up and down the road shake like laughing bodies. Somebody is doing an airy kiss with her lips, the kind of kiss you can't hear, unless you listen very closely.

A young man, clutching flowers, trips and falls. He stands and comes to a thick bush, slows his long strides, and hunkers. His knees are wet and dirty as if sucked on by mouths in the ground. Blood oozes from the palm that stopped his fall. He lays across weeds, his arms beneath him as if they buried him face down. He waters the earth with his tears. A rock points into his ribs.

In the shadow of a rhododendron, somebody shrugs.

There are other people around. They say nothing. They have nothing to say. They don't understand what this is, God bless them.

The young man, something perches on the edge of his lips. It's a kiss. It's a voice.

That day, when it ended, and it was clear that it was over, a moan went out of Tairovsky Cemetery and hitched to the wind, found itself at the Black Sea, where it lassoed onto the motion of the gliding waves. Those waves are never very big, and they die out too soon.

It's the young man's turn to speak. As he speaks, somebody throws her arms heavenward. His voice carries across the granite and marble protrusions. He says something about how mamas make something, and that something goes through this troublesome world, says a few profundities, finger stuck in the air, says even more stupidities, finger stuck higher. That which the mamas make goes across the ocean, does a dance, sings a song, returns to where she came from to find that it's different. The place is different, she's different.

People begin filing away. Somebody *dismissed* somebody else with a *pfft*. The young man and an old man walk deeper into Tairovsky as if they must reach some place not spoken of, impossible to approach in a straight line, a place only found by hearing. Leaves rustle like fingers, gesturing for the two men to approach. Across the sky over the cemetery, the layers that form as the sun moves further west are like strata of soil on the wall of an unearthing. There are random spots where the bottom layer intersects the top and returns back down to the middle. One line jags downward as if into the earth itself. Or maybe it jags upward from the earth. All is as still as the underground.

They return to the grave, do their thing, and, on the way out, "Oof" the young man says. He has struck his head on the iron gate through which one enters the little plot. *Uf*, this young man says. Afterwards, clutching his head, he looks as if he has never said *uf* in his life before and will never say *uf* again. It's as if it was said by an airy gauze.

Now the young man and the old man have come to the sea at the foot of a cliff. They're swimming out to the sea wall, beyond it, floating out there. The young man's face is on the surface, his eyes above, ears beneath. That means he sees one world and hears another.

But the day will come—for the old man first, then the young—when he'll hear both no matter which side he's on. There will no longer be sides. And there will be no more differences.

ACKNOWLEDGEMENTS

Thank you to Natalya Sukhonos, an Odessitka by birth if not altogether by upbringing (and thank God for that?). Thank you Naomi and Nadia, both parts of my heart. Thank you to Suzanne and Ross Singleton and to Chris Singleton. Thank you to all the readers of this manuscript that, along a strange path, made its way to publication. Those readers include: Daniel Nazer; the many members of the San Francisco Writers Workshop in meetings at Alley Cat Books on 14th Street in the Mission; of that cohort, specifically Anna Sears, the moderators Olga Zilberbourg, Judy, Kurt, and James Warner, who read the whole thing early on, thank you; Marina Korenfeld; Lance Hunt; Clare and Loretta of *This Must be the Place*; Michael Collins of *Why There Are Words*; Leland Cheuk; Becca Krock; Mikhail Iossel; and David Bezmozgis.

Thank you, Boris Dralyuk, for reading and taking it seriously and even publishing an excerpt. And thank you to Irina Mashinsky for including that excerpt in *Cardinal Points (Стороны света)*.

Thank you to Kritzler Writers Group: Andres Vaamonde; Taya Kogan; Amy Klein; Ross Barkan; and David Duhr. We sat in a library one night, and the librarian said it sounded like a captivating read. I hope it has been, and if so, you five helped make it that way.

Thank you to all those who inspired this book, including Yan Korenfeld, Pavel and Pavliusha Lumkis, the late Fro Lumkis, the late Aleksandra Tishchenko (Tyotya Sasha), and every Odessan I've encountered. Most important for my understanding of Odessa is, of course, the late Tamara Sukhonos, my mother-in-law. Ваши слова здесь.

Thank you to Thurston Howl Publications for taking it seriously as a work of art.

Thank you to Michael Minayev and M·Graphics as well and for these very pages in the reader's hands.

Thank you, of course, to Bill Ford for these illustrations, bringing the work to life in a way I could not.

Thank you to Josie Schoel for your sensitive edits as well as your friendship over the many years.

Спасибо моей дорогой Марине Эскиной. Спасибо за Ваши дружбу, стихи, страсть к литературе, и то, что Вы представили меня любимой, лучшей учительнице, покойной Галине Шабельской. Мой русский—её чадо. Спасибо, спасибо, спасибо.

Made in the USA
Monee, IL
29 April 2023

32662861R00125